Guilty Knowledge

by

Linda Griffin

Guilty Knowledge

Cover Art by *Abigail Owen*

The Wild Rose Press, Inc.
PO Box 708
Adams Basin, NY 14410-0708
Visit us at www.thewildrosepress.com

Publishing History
First Crimson Rose Edition, 2020
Print ISBN 978-1-5092-3045-7
Digital ISBN 978-1-5092-3046-4

Published in the United States of America

On the ride back to Vista Road, silence prevailed. He didn't know what she was thinking about. He didn't even know what he was thinking about. Lights were on behind the closed curtains of the house. He parked short of the driveway, where the nearest streetlight filled the front seat with a dim glow.

"Thank you," she said. "I enjoyed it, and I appreciate you keeping me up to date on the investigation."

"Is that what I was doing?"

She gave him an enigmatic smile. She had said she found him attractive, but as a kind of conventional compliment. He wondered if she could be as attracted to him as he was to her. He thought yes, but there would be hell to pay if he was wrong—and even if he was right. She was a witness, a lying, maddening witness, and it was unprofessional to think of her in any other way, but something *was* happening between them. He studied the sensitive curve of her slightly parted lips. She had retouched her lipstick in Quique's restroom, a bare hint of color.

He kissed her. Her mouth surprised him, soft and sweet and willing, almost hungry, but with something held back. She was scared, but she wanted this. They were not investigator and witness; they were two people trying to find their way to—what? He didn't know.

Praise for Linda Griffin

"…the author clearly has a handle on the warning signs of emotional abuse—and Teresa is sympathetically drawn… A love story that skillfully shows that abusers don't need to use physical violence to control their victims."

~*Kirkus Reviews*

~*~

"If a romantic suspense is on anyone's wish list, *THE REBOUND EFFECT* should be on that list."

~*InD'Tale Magazine*

~*~

"The sense of danger and the high intensity of the emotions in this book keep you turning the pages… If you are looking for a domestic psychological suspense, this is a fast-paced high intensity read."

~*The Romance Reviews*

~*~

"It was anything but a relaxing read, and my tension was constantly on high alert. …Ms. Griffin's writing style is personal; I was able to feel the characters were real."

~*Tome Tender Book Blog*

Dedication

To Daniel Grubb,
whose advice made this and all my writing better

Acknowledgments

Thanks are owed to my wonderful editor, Nan Swanson, who fights the necessary battles, to Lee Lofland for his excellent book, *Police Procedure & Investigation: A Guide for Writers*, and to the anonymous paramedic who provided information on emergency medicine.

Chapter One

The rain pattered frantically against the third-floor windows of Carroll City Police Headquarters, distracting Jesse from his review of the Thurston case file. Sitting at his desk, he had an unobstructed view of the elevator through the glass wall of the small office, and he saw a young woman emerge. She was damp and flustered, struggling to fasten the strap on her dripping umbrella. Pretty girl, he thought and seconds later couldn't think why. She was white, fairly tall, and slender, with a plain, honest face. Her dark blonde hair fell below her shoulders, and her eyes were wide and dark and slightly slanted. A young Helen Hunt or someone further back, an old-fashioned look. Her clothes were simple: a skirt and sweater and sensible shoes.

She spoke to Michelle at the reception desk, and Michelle, looking bored and critical, pointed to the umbrella stand and then to the open door of the office. The young woman came in but hesitated before she approached his desk. "Detective Aaron?"

"That's right," he said. "Jesse Aaron." He stood up and held out his hand. She shook it briefly, her fingers slim and cool in his. "How can I help you?"

"I have some information about a crime," she said.

"Okay. Have a seat." He indicated the chair across from him, and she sat primly, knees together, small handbag clutched in her lap. He sat down, pulled a notebook and pen toward him, and began with the obvious: "Your name?"

She took a deep breath and said what sounded like, "Suh-ry-ah Brennan."

"S-u...?"

"S-a-r-i-a-h."

She seemed to need prompting. "You have some information, Ms. Brennan?" She wasn't as eager to spill her secret as most informants—did she have a reason to hold back?

"About a murder. They said you were investigating it. Rosa Logan." Her voice was soft and unhurried.

"Yes?" He kept his tone even. If she expected a reaction, she would be disappointed. A hundred telephone tips had come in on the case before the blood was dry at the crime scene, but to have someone sent upstairs to speak to him was unusual. Rosa Logan had been twenty-three, attractive, blonde, and pink-cheeked. Now she was dead, her skull caved in, her throat slashed. He hadn't been able to shake the image of her staring eyes and her bright hair darkened with blood. It was a nasty case with no easy answers.

"I know who did it," Sariah Brennan said.

"Uh-huh. Who's that?" He had heard this before. The last one had been certain her dentist committed the murder. Most tips were a waste of time, but checking them out was a necessary part of the job.

"I don't know his full name, but he's called Casey. A big, dark man with a scar on his neck."

Yes, wasn't it always a big, dark man? "Dark-skinned?"

"Dark hair, dark clothes. His complexion...about

2

as dark as you, but not African-American."

"Latino, Middle Eastern…?"

"I don't think so. Maybe Slavic or Eastern European."

"And you know this how?" Jesse jotted the keywords in his notebook and didn't realize immediately that she hadn't answered. He looked up. "Ms. Brennan?" Her reluctance to explain was unusual, and his experience-honed instincts told him she was hiding something or knew more than she should.

"I saw him…in my head, like in a vision."

"I see." One of those, although she didn't seem the type. He put down his pen. Department policy was to check out even this kind of tip if it was specific enough, but he had never seen one lead anywhere. She was a little flushed now, but her gaze remained steady, her chin up. He tried to keep the skepticism out of his voice as he asked, "So you're a psychic? You get these visions all the time?"

"No," she said. "Only one other time, when I was fourteen. My brother fell in a well, and I knew what happened and brought help, even though I was too far away to hear him calling. My grandmother said I had a gift but I should keep quiet about it."

"And did you?"

"Until today." She gave him a direct, challenging look. "I know this man Casey killed Rosa Logan."

"Did you know her?"

"No."

"But it came to you that she was killed by a man with a scar on his neck?" He still had a nagging feeling that she knew something, but surely this wasn't how.

"Yes. I know how it sounds, but I had to tell you,

3

because there's another one. If you don't stop him, he'll kill her too."

"Who? Is it you?" She gave a short, surprised laugh. "If it is, we can protect you. You don't have to be afraid."

"What are you going to do—to find him?"

He gave her the standard answer: "We're following up a lot of leads," and added, "I'll run this description through the local and NCIC databases and ask her associates if they recognize it." He picked up his pen again. "Can you describe the scar?"

"A red mark about an inch high." She touched the left side of her neck. "Here. It was like a C, a backwards C."

Jesse wrote that down. "Okay. Thanks." He handed her a card from the holder on the desk. "If you think of anything else, you can call me." He meant it as a dismissal, but she didn't leave.

"He…He took one of her fingers in his mouth. After she was dead."

The hair on the back of his neck prickled, but he remained expressionless. "In his mouth? Which finger?"

"I'm not sure. I think it was her left hand."

"Were you there?" She must have been. Unless she had a source inside the investigation, in which case someone should be fired, she was an eyewitness. How else could she have known Rosa Logan's ring finger had teeth marks on it? The theory was that the killer had used his teeth to pull off her wedding ring, but the information hadn't been released to the media.

"Only in my head." Her eyes did not waver from his. "Do you believe me?"

He shrugged, although of course he didn't. "That's above my pay grade," he said. "It's not my job to believe or disbelieve. How do you know there will be another victim?" He didn't believe she'd had a vision, but he no longer wanted to dismiss her.

She shrugged. "There will be," she said with quiet confidence, "if you don't stop him."

"We'll do our best. I'm going to need your contact information."

She gave him a phone number, but before he could prompt her for her address, Camille strode in, bringing with her a gust of cold air and all of her usual energy. Jesse stood up, feeling a need to blunt the impact of her personality on this questionable witness.

"My partner, Detective Camille Farris," he said and gave Camille a look he hoped would suggest finesse was required. "This is Sariah Brennan. She has some information in the Rosa Logan case."

"You won't believe me," Ms. Brennan said bluntly, "but it's true."

"Why wouldn't we believe you?" Camille asked, glaring at her. Her tone suggested she was sure they would find a good reason not to. She was a formidable woman, nearly six feet tall and broad-shouldered, not unfeminine but tough-looking. She wore her hair in a very short Afro style and dressed in no-nonsense trousers, shirts, and jackets. Not many people were willing to mess with her.

"I saw it," Ms. Brennan said, "in my head."

"Oh, yeah?" Camille challenged. "Saw what?"

"He put her finger in his mouth." Although Jesse had tried not to reveal anything, she knew it was the crucial piece of information.

His partner had a better poker face than he did. "You buying that?" she asked him.

"I've got this," he said.

Camille started to say something to the young woman and then glanced at him instead. "I'll—" She pointed to her own desk. He nodded, and she marched away.

"You know him, don't you?" he asked Ms. Brennan.

She shook her head.

"You know something more, though," he insisted. She didn't answer and glanced in Camille's direction. "Maybe we should talk somewhere a little more private?" he suggested.

"Where?" A hint of apprehension colored her voice.

He gestured toward the interrogation room with its reinforced glass window and heavy door. "Nobody can overhear us in there." He didn't mention the video camera installed above the door.

She stood up, clutching her purse. He took that as assent and led the way. As they passed Camille's desk, he tore a page from his notebook and left it with her. She would put the name and description into the local crime database and see what came up. He stopped at the coffee urn to fill two cups and gestured for Ms. Brennan to enter and take a seat. Before she settled into the chair, she glanced out the window, as if to be sure she could be seen.

"We don't use rubber hoses," he assured her, taking the seat opposite.

"I'm sorry," she said. "I'm not used to being alone in a room with someone I don't know." He supposed *someone* meant a man or maybe a black man.

"I'm actually a pretty nice guy," he said, smiling, and then, speaking casually to put her at ease, "Sariah is an unusual name. Where does it come from?"

"Sariah was a woman of great faith," she said. The words sounded rote, like a quotation. "She might be the only good woman mentioned by name in the Book of Mormon."

Jesse sat back, interested now. "Are you Mormon?" It would explain a lot.

"No," she said. "Yours is from the Old Testament. Are you Jewish?"

"No. Point taken." He sipped his coffee and studied her.

She took a tentative taste of hers. "Bitter," she said.

He indicated the packets on the desk. "Sugar might help. I can get you a soda from the machine, if you'd prefer."

"This is fine. Ask your questions." Her voice had taken on a steely tone.

"Okay. I have to ask this first, to get it out of the way. It doesn't mean I believe you've done anything wrong. Where were you on the night of February fifth?"

"Home."

"Which is...?"

"I live in an apartment above a garage. 4763 Vista Road."

"Anybody see you there that night?"

"Not that I remember. The people in the house might have seen my lights."

"Tell me about your vision," he suggested. "Was it like a dream?"

"No. I was awake."

"But you saw things, like in a dream? Images? Did you hear voices?"

"No."

"How did you know his name was Casey?"

She shrugged. "I just knew."

"And you saw him kill her?"

"No. I saw a lot of blood, and I knew he had killed her. I saw him put her finger in his mouth."

"Could you tell where they were?"

"A big, empty building." It was a reasonable description of the warehouse, but she could have found the information in the media reports. She looked away, out the window again.

"I'm sorry if I'm making you nervous," he said. "First time in a police station?"

"Yes, but you've been very kind. I didn't know if anybody would even listen."

"And you don't know anybody else you could have told? Nobody connected to the police or the case?"

She wasn't fooled. "You're trying to find out where the leak was. There's no leak. It's just me."

"Sorry," he said. "I'm usually smoother. What else can you tell me about Casey? You said dark hair—long, short?"

"Short, neatly trimmed, a little curly."

"And his clothes?"

"Dark jacket and trousers."

"Style? Material?"

"Nothing distinctive."

"It's not much, but we'll see what we can come up with. Do you think you could pick out features for a sketch?" She shook her head. "Could you pick him out of a lineup?"

8

"I don't think so. I didn't see his face clearly."

"And his name—Casey? First or last?"

"I don't know. Just Casey."

"What about her? Did you know her name?"

"Not until I read it in the paper." Out of questions, Jesse put down his pen and sat back. "You don't believe me," she said, "but you're being very polite about it."

"I try," he said, but the truth was he didn't always try this hard. There was something oddly plausible about this young woman. He glanced through the window to where Camille sat at her desk. She was on the computer, and she wasn't very happy. Ms. Brennan looked too, and he said, "We don't play good cop, bad cop, but if Detective Farris isn't satisfied with what I get, she'll want to have a turn. She has a way of getting what she wants. It would be easier for both of us if you tell me how you came by this information."

She looked at him gravely. "That's not good cop, bad cop?" she asked.

He had to laugh. "Yeah, okay. You got me." He was looking at her, but out of the corner of his eye he saw Camille go to the printer and then come toward the interrogation room. "Uh-oh," he said.

Ms. Brennan looked. "Bad cop," she said.

Camille yanked open the door, strode in, and slapped four sheets of paper on the table in front of Ms. Brennan. "Any of these look like him?"

She glanced down and then leaned forward to take a closer look. One hand covered her mouth as she pointed to the picture on the far right. Jesse picked it up. It was a standard mug shot: two photos, face front and profile, of a middle-aged man. The profile view showed a semi-circular red scar on his neck. He had dark, curly hair and dark eyes, a long face, large features, and a prominent nose. Those characteristics could arguably be called Slavic, but his skin was darker than most Europeans. Jesse glanced at the other three pictures—all of dark men with similar scars—and handed the one she had singled out to Ms. Brennan. "Look again. You think that's him? Even though you didn't see his face very well?"

"Yes. His hair was a little shorter, but I'm sure it's him."

Camille snatched the mug shot out of her hand. "If you're through wasting our time, we have work to do," she said. "Get out of here."

"I know I'm right," Ms. Brennan said, but she stood up.

"Good for you," Camille said, "but don't screw up this investigation. If you tell anyone anything we discussed here, you can be charged with obstructing justice. In fact, we could charge you right now for filing a false report."

"I'm right," she repeated, speaking only to Jesse, but she edged past Camille and left the room. She hurried to the elevator, almost forgetting her umbrella in her haste.

Jesse looked up at his partner. "Damn it, Camille! What did you do that for? She did know about the teeth marks. You can't just brush that off."

"Somebody told her or she overheard it," she said. "A source in the department or somebody associated with the killer. Check her out. Does she have a police record? Make a complaint recently? Ever try this before? You know the drill. Find out who she knows,

10

who she hangs out with, but don't believe anything *she* says."

"She identified a suspect. However she found out, she knows who did it."

"She's lying. She made up this vision crap to get attention, or if she knows something, to mislead us." She dropped the mug shot Brennan had chosen on the table, dismissing it.

"One of Logan's co-workers might be able to identify him," Jesse said.

"It's not him."

"Why not? Who is he?"

She consulted her notebook. "His name is Kazimir Capek."

"K.C.," he said. "Casey." He assumed the other three were also called Casey, but it still felt like a confirmation.

"Sounds like our suspect, hunh?" Camille snapped. "Only trouble is—the dude is dead. He died three years ago."

Chapter Two

Jesse tried to hide his surprise. "It's not the first time a witness has identified the wrong man," he said. "I still think she knows something."

"She's a friggin' wacko."

"I don't know," he demurred. "I kind of liked her."

"Oh, you *liked* her? Well, as long as you *liked* her. You are such a pussy, Aaron."

"And you scare people off. Now I'll have to talk to her again."

"Poor you."

"It's not like we have anything else," he pointed out. "No fingerprints, no DNA match, nobody who knew the victim well. None of the other tips made any sense at all."

The lock on the back alley door to the warehouse had been broken, but the single surveillance camera at the street entrance had revealed nothing. So far Rosa Logan had proved to have only casual acquaintances—her immediate neighbors, landlady, supervisor, and a few co-workers. They knew only that she was a widow, new in town, worked hard, and paid her rent on time. She had a Social Security card but hadn't reported any earnings to SSA or the IRS before the previous year. She had probably changed her identity. Her apartment was clean. She owned a car, but it had been in the shop at the time of the murder.

Jesse sighed. "Any luck with the pawn shops?"

"None. If the wacko won't tell you who her source is, we'll have to do it the hard way. And don't think I don't know why you like her. If she was some ugly old hag, you wouldn't believe her."

"I don't believe her anyway."

"You want to, though."

He didn't have to answer, because Michelle put through a call, and he went out to his desk to answer it. The caller was Libby Gaynor, one of Rosa Logan's co-workers at Delondra's Pizza. They had been waiting for next-of-kin to be located, but none had surfaced, and now Gaynor had decided to make the necessary arrangements. The memorial service would be a very modest affair at the church she attended, but she understood the detectives wanted to be present. "I don't know if anybody else will," she confessed. "I promised the minister it wouldn't be publicized. They don't want a lot of reporters and curiosity seekers showing up, so I only told her neighbors and the other people at work. I don't know if they'll come or not. It's tomorrow at two p.m. The Church of Christ on Hughes Avenue." Jesse would have preferred something more public, but if the killer was someone close to Logan, he might still hear about it and turn up.

****

He wore his one good black suit for the service, hoping not to stand out in the expected small group of mourners. Camille smirked at him. "You look like an undertaker," she said.

"That seems appropriate," he said mildly. They were in his black Interceptor, because her car would stand out more—she opted for style over discretion in a cherry-red Chrysler. Using her remark as an excuse, he glanced at his reflection in the sun visor mirror before he started the car.

"Stop worrying about your hair," she ordered.

"I'm not," he said, but he was. Was his hairline receding?

Camille snorted. "It's fine."

"Maybe I'll shave my head."

"Like that'll be an improvement. Bald is sexy, though."

"Is it? I could be Michael Jordan."

"Yeah, or Kojak."

The Church of Christ on Hughes Avenue was a modest building with a simple, tasteful cross above the door and a projection on the roof that could barely be called a steeple. Five cars were parked in the small lot, and Camille took down their license numbers before Jesse pulled in at the end of the row.

The nave was dimly lit, and the organist played soft music as they entered. A simply framed eight-by-ten of Rosa Logan, on a small easel, and a modest arrangement of white lilies, roses, and chrysanthemums were the only ornaments. The room was almost empty, with the few present clustered in the first three rows of pews. Aside from Jesse and Camille, the only person of color was a slender, young Latino they had spoken to at Delondra's. All the other mourners were female, and only one was unfamiliar—an older woman who sat with Libby Gaynor, possibly her mother. Not a promising group in which to find a killer. None of them was strong enough to have bashed Logan's head in. Jesse and Camille sat behind them in the fourth row. They might have looked like a married couple, but everybody would know they were the police.

The service was short and impersonal, with a couple of hymns to add a proper gravitas. When it was over, Libby Gaynor came up to thank them for attending, as if she didn't know they had ulterior motives. There was no sign of a likely suspect, but Jesse left secretly more disappointed by Sariah Brennan's absence. If she didn't know Rosa Logan, she wouldn't even have heard about it, but she might have made things more interesting.

****

4763 Vista Road was in an older neighborhood of single family homes on tree-lined streets feeding into busy Hawley Boulevard. The house was well maintained, with a green lawn and window boxes full of flowers. Narrow wooden stairs led to the apartment above the two-car garage. Jesse parked on the street and went first to the front door of the house, guessing Sariah Brennan was still at work.

The doorbell was answered by a slender, blonde woman in slacks and a long-sleeved blouse. She was fortyish, with too much makeup and an automatic smile. "Good afternoon," she said. Jesse showed her his badge, and the smile didn't waver. "My goodness," she said.

"Detective Aaron," he said. "I'm sorry to bother you, but I'm conducting a routine investigation and need to ask you a few questions about your tenant."

"Sariah? She can't be in any trouble with the police, surely."

"Not at all, but she might be a witness to a crime."

"She hasn't said anything about it to me."

"Are you close?"

"Oh, I suppose not," the woman admitted. "She's a nice girl, but keeps to herself. I'm sorry; would you like to come in?"

"Thank you, ma'am."

"Oh, it's Peggy," she said, laughing. "Peggy Dunwood." She led the way into a neat, tastefully furnished living room and gestured toward an armchair. "Would you like something to drink?" she offered.

"No, thank you." He sat down, and she perched on the edge of the couch with her hands on her knees, looking bright and expectant. He got down to business. "How long has Ms. Brennan been living above the garage?"

"Four months now, I guess."

"Do you know where she lived before?"

"She gave me the address so I could check her references, but I forget—Orchard Street, something like that."

"Do you know where she works?"

"Let's see… She said it was a new job. Something with animals? Not a veterinarian—a pet shop? You'd have to ask her."

"I will. What time does she usually get home, do you know?"

She glanced at her watch. "It's not like I check up on her or anything, you know, but I think it varies. Errands after work and so on. Five or six, maybe."

"Do you happen to remember seeing her on February fifth?"

"February fifth?" She looked blank. "What day of the week was it?"

"Wednesday. A week ago Wednesday."

"Oh, okay, the day the heating guy was here. I

16

don't think I saw her come home from work, but I know she was there later. Again, I wasn't checking on her; I happened to see lights on when I put the trash bins out. Thursday is trash day. Does she need an alibi or something?"

"No, not at all. Just double-checking our facts. You don't know her well, but you would have expected her to mention it to you if she witnessed a crime?"

"It would be pretty exciting, wouldn't it? I'd sure want to tell people if it was me."

"Only natural," he agreed.

"Of course, I mostly talk to her when she pays the rent and stuff like that, but we have had a few nice chats. What kind of crime was it?" She leaned forward, eyes alight with eager interest.

"I can't discuss the case right now. Does she have any frequent visitors?"

"I don't know that I've ever seen anybody."

"Has she ever mentioned to you anything about having special abilities?"

"Special abilities? My goodness. What do you mean? Sounds kinky!"

"So that's a no?"

"Special abilities? No, I can't think of anything like that. My goodness!"

"Okay, thank you. You've been very helpful, ma'am." He closed his notebook and stood up.

"It's Peggy." She stood up more slowly and put her hand on his arm. "If you're waiting for her to come home, would you like to stay and have a drink? It's about that time for me."

"Not while I'm on duty."

"Of course. A club soda, then? My husband won't

be home until seven or eight. We could talk about *your* special abilities, Mister Detective."

"Detective Aaron," he corrected her. "Thank you for your help…Peggy."

He beat a hasty retreat and sat in the car until Ms. Brennan came around the corner, carrying a paper grocery bag. She wore a pink smock that put him in mind of hospital candy stripers. She was almost to the stairs when he got out and approached her. "Can I help you carry that?" he asked. She looked startled, and he added a hasty, "Sorry." Thinking she might not remember him, he showed her his badge. "Detective Aaron."

"Yes, I remember," she said. "Why are you here?"

"I have a few more questions."

"I gave you my phone number. You could have called and asked your questions, or I would have come in."

"I'm sorry if this isn't a convenient time, but it won't take long. Are you sure I can't help you with the bag? It looks heavy."

"It's not." She stood where she was, making no move to climb the stairs. "Ask your questions."

"Here?" He waited for her to invite him up to her apartment. She didn't. She glanced around, shrugged, and shifted the weight of her groceries a little. "Is there a reason you don't want me to see where you live?" he asked.

"Yes." He raised his eyebrows, and after a perceptible pause she added, "I'm a very private person. So unless you have a search warrant…"

"You contacted us," he reminded her. He could see she wasn't going to budge. "Okay, go put your groceries away. I'll wait."

She hesitated a little longer before she climbed the stairs. They were fairly steep, and this woman must be in good shape if she went up and down them every day. Jesse leaned against the Interceptor with his arms folded and waited. Out of the corner of his eye he saw curtains flutter in a front window of the house. Peggy Dunwood was watching.

Ms. Brennan was gone a good ten minutes. She came back in new-looking navy jeans and a blue pullover sweater, with her hair neatly combed. She looked very put together and pretty, not sexy exactly, but appealing in a way that made him feel protective. "All right," she said in a stern, challenging voice. "Ask your questions."

"Boy, you are tough," he complained. "Can we at least sit down? In the car if you insist, or I think I saw a Java Prince up on Hawley." She didn't respond, studying him gravely. "I'll buy you a cup of coffee," he offered.

"Like a date?" she asked. "Shouldn't we keep this professional?"

He had to laugh, and she showed a flicker of response. "Pay for your own coffee, then."

She took a deep breath. "All right. Java Prince."

The walk was short, and she kept her head down and her hands in her pockets. Jesse had momentarily forgotten the questions he wanted to ask her. Finally he said, "I talked to your landlady. She did see your lights the night of the murder."

She looked up. "What did you tell her?"

"Nothing. Or just that you might be a witness to a crime."

"Thank you."

The Java Prince was festooned with paper hearts for Valentine's Day, which he had done his best to ignore. It was crowded, but he spotted an empty table near the back and gestured to her to take it. "What would you like?" he asked.

"I have no idea," she confessed. "You choose." She went to the table, and he joined the line. What would she like? Most women liked chocolate, many were calorie conscious, and it was best to keep it simple. He ordered a medium light mocha for her, French roast for himself, and two slices of low-fat chocolate banana coffee cake. Even the cups were festive, decorated with hearts and words in a childish design.

He set the mocha in front of her, and she looked at it dubiously. "This is coffee?"

"Yes, it's definitely coffee. It has chocolate syrup in it and hot milk—all low fat, I promise. The cake is low fat too."

"I thought police officers ate doughnuts."

"Ancient stereotype," he said, but he smiled to show he wasn't offended. She smiled back as if she was amused by something. "What?" he asked.

"You have a nice smile."

"Thank you. I thought you wanted to be professional about this."

"I do." She took a cautious sip. He noticed she wore little or no makeup, but her skin was flawless. "This is good," she said politely.

"Not really into the Java Prince experience, are you?"

She looked blank, as if she didn't know what he meant. "Don't you have some questions to ask? You said it wouldn't take long." She tapped the heart design on her cup. "It's Valentine's Day. I'd think you'd have better things to do."

"I'm sorry; do you have a date?"

"I have plans," she said. A bit evasive, but none of his business.

"Why did you identify that mug shot?" he asked abruptly, before she could be braced for the question. He was about to stray from procedure, but he needed a straight answer.

She blinked. "I saw him."

"In your head."

"Yes."

"Unfortunately, the man you identified is dead."

She was taken aback, but didn't waver. "He wasn't when he killed her," she said.

"He died three years ago."

She shook her head. "Why did Detective Farris show me his picture, then?"

"She showed you men who fit the description you gave and had the name or nickname Casey. Sometimes we use obviously impossible suspects just to fill out the array. I can't tell you his name, but he was arrested for assault seven years ago. The charges were dropped, and no DNA sample was taken. He had no other police record. He died three years ago of cardiovascular disease, although he was only fifty-two."

"I don't think so."

"Everybody else seems to be convinced. His wife is receiving death benefit payments from his life insurance. Insurance companies require death certificates."

"They can be faked. He's still alive, and he killed

Rosa Logan."

"Maybe it was someone else, not Rosa Logan, in your…vision."

"Don't say it like that," she said.

Jesse shrugged. "I don't want to be disrespectful, but…it's a stretch."

"It was Rosa Logan and the man called Casey. The man in the picture."

"I'm afraid not. The most likely explanation is that you were mistaken or whatever you saw wasn't real. Or you're lying and wasting everybody's time. It would be easy to dismiss, but we need to know how you knew the killer put her finger in his mouth."

"I told you how."

"Why do you think he did it?"

"I don't know. I thought it was a strange thing to do."

"Do you know how we knew he did it?"

"How would I know that? How *did* you know? DNA on her finger?"

"If you really don't know, I'd better not tell you."

"Bad cop wouldn't like it?" she suggested.

He let that go. "The information hasn't been released to the media and won't be. So here we have a witness who knows this little detail, but identifies a dead man as the killer. What would you think?"

"I'd think he wasn't dead."

"Yeah, well, he is. We'll double check with the insurance company, but they don't like to hand out money without proof. Now, if you claimed to have seen the murder take place or if you'd seen this suspect in the flesh…"

"So you would rather I lied?"

"Would it be a lie?"

Her gaze didn't waver, but she didn't answer. She drank her coffee in a silence emphasized by the buzz of voices around them. "I've told you everything I can," she said. "I'm not sorry I went to see you, but I'm sorry you don't believe me, because you need to stop him."

"Because you think there's another victim? Do you know who it is?"

"No. Another woman is all I know."

"Have you learned anything else since the first…vision or whatever?" She shook her head. "Excuse me for saying so, but you don't act much like a person with psychic abilities."

"Have you met a lot of them? How do they act?"

"For starters, they have these experiences more than every decade or so, and they've usually told other people about them. Someone who wants to give the police information without revealing how she got it and pretends to be psychic, on the other hand…"

"I see." She sipped her coffee and said nothing else for a long time. He kept silent too, waiting to see if she would confess. "This *is* good," she said finally. "Why does it have all this foam on top?"

"Where did you grow up?" he asked. It wasn't a non sequitur—didn't even small towns have Java Prince franchises these days?

Apparently she understood how he meant it. "I don't usually drink coffee," she said.

"So why now?"

She hesitated. "When in Rome? You drink it. I'm trying to fit in."

"Seriously? Where are you from—Mars?"

She laughed. It did amazing things for her, gave a

pretty flush of color to her pale skin, softened the lines of her face, and revealed her straight, even teeth. "Something like that," she said.

"So—what? You thought I'd be more likely to believe you if you were…"

"Less like a Martian? What *would* make you believe me?"

"Tell me how you knew he put her finger in his mouth."

"I saw it. I wasn't at the warehouse, so…"

"You must be psychic."

"You say you don't believe me, but you came to where I live to ask me about it again. Why not dismiss me as a crazy person?"

"We need to know how you knew."

"You're wasting your time when you should be trying to find Casey."

"Where would you suggest I look?"

"You want me to tell you how to do your job?"

"No, I think I can handle it." He changed tack. "Are you on any medication?"

"Medication? No. I wasn't hallucinating, if that's what you're suggesting. I don't even take aspirin. I don't drink alcohol, either, and I don't normally drink coffee. No chemicals were involved." She sipped her coffee and waited for the next question.

Jesse didn't have one. "You should try some of this cake," he suggested.

"It would spoil my dinner. Don't you have to get home to your wife and children?"

"No wife. No children."

"Your girlfriend, then. You must have one."

"No, not right now." She raised her eyebrows,

clearly skeptical. "Cops don't make good domestic partners," he said.

"Do you at least have a dog? Go home and feed your dog."

"No, my last girlfriend got custody of the dog. But I did promise this wouldn't take long, so I'll walk you home as soon as you're ready."

"Stop trying to be nice to me."

"Why shouldn't I be nice to you? I'm the good cop, remember?"

"You don't believe my story, and I'm…not like the women you're used to."

"Meaning what?"

"They know how to flirt and wear makeup and so on."

"Did you think I was flirting with you?"

"No, of course not. You don't have to take me home, either. I didn't bring any money, but I'll pay you back for the coffee. How much was it?"

"This one's on me. All I ask is that you think about helping me out by telling the truth about what you know." She opened her mouth to respond, and he put up a hand to forestall her. "Just think about it. And of course don't tell anybody what we talked about; Detective Farris's warning still applies. You can call me anytime. Otherwise I'll have to talk to everybody you know, and I can't promise to be as discreet as I was with the landlady. She told me where you work, so I'll start there."

"I didn't tell her where…or maybe I did." She bit her lip.

"I have it right here," he said, patting the pocket he had slid his notebook into. "Pet store, isn't it?"

"Please don't go there. I need the job, and you'll make me sound like a nut case."

"You are a nut case," he said, smiling.

"I've told you everything," she said. "I was only trying to help. I haven't done anything wrong."

"Okay. Think about it. Call me." He folded a napkin around the untouched piece of coffee cake. "You can have it for dessert or for breakfast," he said. "Put it in the microwave for ten seconds or so. It tastes better warm. You do have a microwave?"

"Yes," she said sharply, angry now for some reason, her cheeks a little flushed. "I have a microwave." She took the napkin out of his hand and got up to leave.

"Don't go away mad," he said mildly.

"I can't tell whether you're making fun of me or not," she complained, and then she was gone. Jesse sat at the table a little longer, warming his hands against the cup with its Java Prince logo and Valentine's Day hearts and wondering—not what she was hiding, but why he wanted to believe her.

Chapter Three

Peggy Dunwood hadn't told Jesse the name of the pet store, but a little routine detective work with state employment records uncovered World of Wings on the recently renamed Obama Street. The small shop was squeezed between a mom-and-pop restaurant and an Afrocentric barbershop. When he opened the door on Saturday morning, he was met with a cacophony of varied bird song and the musky odor of damp feathers. Cages were everywhere, and large cockatoos and brightly colored macaws sat on perches—enough birds to cast a Hitchcock movie.

A brown-haired woman in her forties approached him at once. She looked a little harassed, but she smiled and greeted him warmly. "Welcome to World of Wings. What can I help you with?"

Jesse showed her his badge. Her smile faded. "Is something wrong?" she asked.

"I hope not," he said. "Is Ms. Brennan here?"

"No, I'm sorry; this is her day off, but I'm sure I can help you," she said, falling back into salesperson mode.

"I'm sure you can," he said. "I'm just verifying Ms. Brennan's employment."

"Why? Is she in trouble?"

"No, nothing like that."

"She's a very good employee," the woman

hastened to assure him. "I trust her completely, and I don't understand why her last employer didn't. Sariah said it was a misunderstanding, and I'm sure it was. Is that what this is about?"

"Her last employer? That would be…?"

"The department store—Maxine's." She frowned. "Maybe you should ask her about it; I don't want to talk about her behind her back."

"I understand," he said. "This is just routine fact-checking. You've confirmed she works here, and I gather she's punctual, dependable. Are there other employees working here that I might talk to?"

"No, it's just the two of us. All I can afford, I'm afraid."

"Anybody ever visit her here? Come by to chat, take her to lunch?"

"Not when I was here."

"Did she tell you what she might have seen?"

"No, what? Here, you mean?"

"No, no, and we're not even sure what she witnessed is significant. You'd be surprised how repetitive and boring police work can be."

Reassured, she said, "Try feeding a hundred birds every day. They're wonderful companions, though—could I interest you in a sweet little songbird? They're very easy pets to care for and very cheerful and friendly. If you have children, it's a good way to teach them responsibility without a lot of fuss and bother."

"Thank you, but—"

"*Do* you have children?"

"No, no children."

"If you live alone, a bird makes a cheerful noise in the house. A sure cure for depression."

Jesse wasn't depressed, but he wondered if something about him suggested he lived alone. Before he could excuse himself, there was a blur of movement behind him, and something settled on his shoulder. It was a parrot with a large beak, a long tail, and blue and gold feathers.

"She likes you," the shop owner said, but apparently she could see how uncomfortable he was and coaxed the bird back onto a perch. "This is Tango," she said. "She's a macaw, a very popular breed because they can talk and they easily bond with people. They're very intelligent. Isn't she beautiful?"

Jesse had to agree.

Tango responded with an ear-splitting screech.

"That is one drawback," the woman said, laughing. "They do make a lot of noise sometimes. Maybe you would prefer a nice canary or a parakeet?"

"I work crazy hours sometimes, so it isn't very practical for me to have a pet."

"One bird is no trouble at all. Mind you, keeping up with all of these"—she gestured to include the entire shop—"is quite a job, but one is nothing."

"And Ms. Brennan helps you with them?"

"Yes, the feeding and cleaning cages and so on— she's very diligent and not a bad saleswoman, either." She opened the door of a nearby cage, and a canary hopped onto her finger. "Isn't he sweet?" she said coaxingly.

"Uh, yes," he said, "but I'm afraid I have to go now."

"Oh, well, come back anytime and take a better look," she suggested. She put the canary back in the cage. "Sariah is particularly good with the small ones," she said. "They really take to her."

"Maybe she has a psychic gift or something."

"Hardly that," the shop owner said, "but perhaps a certain sympathy for the small and helpless." Which didn't suggest Brennan had claimed to be psychic here either.

Maxine's was his next stop. There were two stores in town, and he started with the one nearest Sariah Brennan's apartment. They had no record of her having ever been employed and suggested he check with corporate headquarters. Instead he headed for the other store. When he drove past the warehouse district, he realized this Maxine's was only a few blocks from the Logan crime scene, in Plaza Center, a medium-sized mall of similar department stores and specialty shops.

He asked for directions to the personnel office and was told they weren't hiring. The young woman glared at him disapprovingly, and it was a particular satisfaction to show her his badge. "I can call the security guard for you," she offered, "if it's about shoplifting."

"It's about murder," he said. He couldn't resist.

"Oh, um…second floor, next to the salon. It says Staff Only, but you can knock."

By the time he got to the second floor, the young woman had called ahead to say he was on the way, and a light-skinned African-American woman in a conservative suit and high heels met him at the door. He flashed his badge, and she said, "Detective," brusquely and ushered him inside. The office was nicer than he expected, as if somebody had taken considerable care with its furnishings. She gestured to the visitor's chair, which proved firm but comfortable, and settled herself behind her desk with her hands folded on it. "What can I help you with?" she asked.

"I'm here to ask about a former employee, Sariah Brennan."

He expected her to consult her records, but she registered instant recognition. "Oh, *her,*" she said scathingly. "She was dismissed for good cause, no matter what she says. It isn't a criminal matter, and if she wants to take it to court, we are fully prepared to defend the case."

"All I want is to confirm that she worked here. I guess there was a problem?"

"We certainly wouldn't give her a good reference. What does this have to do with the police?"

"It's part of a routine investigation. What was the problem with Ms. Brennan?"

"I don't think I can discuss it with you," she said. "If she wants to get ugly about this, her lawyer can contact our legal department."

"I don't need to get involved in a labor dispute," he said. "Ms. Brennan may be a witness in a criminal case, and I'm trying to find out how reliable she might be."

"I wouldn't believe a word she says," the woman snapped.

"Was she friendly with any other employees here?"

"Not to my knowledge."

"Did she ever have a friend visit her at work?"

"We discourage that. If there's anything *else* I can help you with..." She stood up, already eager to usher him out.

He now had two contrasting views of Sariah Brennan: model employee with a sympathetic gift, and difficult, unreliable liar. She couldn't be a genuine psychic—there was no such thing—and was probably guilty of something related to the Logan case. He was more intrigued than ever with the mystery surrounding her.

Chapter Four

Jesse saw Sariah get off the elevator again on Monday morning. It wasn't raining this time, and she was less tentative—and twice as pretty. She might have been wearing lipstick, maybe even a touch of blush, but he didn't think makeup was the reason. She came in through the open door and straight to his desk and put down a handful of bills and change. If he wasn't mistaken, it was exactly the price of a medium mocha and a slice of coffee cake. She must have gone back to the Java Prince to find out.

"You didn't have to pay me back," he said.

"Yes, I did," she said firmly and added indignantly, "It kept me awake."

"Something else probably kept you awake. Guilty conscience maybe?"

"How did *you* sleep?" she challenged him. "You lied to me."

He didn't deny it. "It takes a liar to know a liar, or so they say."

"Peggy told me she didn't tell you where I worked."

"Didn't she? I'm sure she was the one who mentioned the pet shop. You didn't tell me you used to work near where Rosa Logan was killed."

She was surprised, but not dismayed. "You've been investigating *me*? It's a waste of time. I worked in that part of town—I didn't know it was near where she was killed—and it was months ago."

"So I understand. What happened at Maxine's?"

"Nothing happened. It was a misunderstanding."

"A serious one, apparently." She didn't respond. "Did you come in here just to pay me back and call me a liar?" he asked.

"I want to know what you're doing to find the killer."

"Does that mean you're not so sure it was the man you identified?"

"No. It was him." Anger, not cosmetics, put the color in her cheeks.

"As a matter of fact, I was thinking about calling you. I have a few more questions."

She surveyed the room. "Bad cop isn't here?"

Jesse glanced toward Michelle at the reception desk. She was on the phone. "You'd better not let anyone else hear you call her that. She happens to be an excellent detective, and she has to act twice as tough as the rest of us because she's a woman." He got up to close the office door, and Sariah sat down without being prompted.

"This is why I was going to call you," he said, indicating the folder he had been studying. "A good DNA sample was obtained from the victim's finger, as you guessed, but no match was found in the database. So we sent it to the FBI lab for further analysis. You'd be surprised what they can learn from a little smear of saliva."

"What the killer looked like?"

"No. Maybe someday we'll be able to, though. It's a new science, improving all the time. It used to take weeks to get any information at all. Now you can get a match almost overnight. If no exact match is found, sometimes one will be close enough to suggest a family relationship, and we can interview the relatives. There's also a test now for eye color, which is supposed to be fairly reliable, and they can often tell the person's geographic origin." He tapped the folder.

She sat forward, intent on his face. "What did they find?"

"You already know, don't you?"

She shook her head.

"The killer had dark brown eyes and, although this is more subjective, it's highly probable that his ancestors were from both Eastern Europe and Northern Africa."

"I told you," she said.

"It gets even better."

"What do you mean? They found a relative?"

"No, he apparently came from a law-abiding family, at least recently. He, however, may be guilty of a number of crimes, including insurance fraud." She started to speak, and he raised his hand. "*May* be. We spoke to the agent who handled his widow's claim. He insisted the case was perfectly straightforward and legitimate, but he was very defensive. He admitted we were not the first to question the validity of the death certificate. Further investigation is called for."

"I knew it." She was triumphant.

"Yes. The question is how? I think you have what we call guilty knowledge. Either you were at the scene or you had some contact with the killer afterward."

She shook her head. "I was at home that night. Peggy told you I was."

"No, she said she saw your lights. You could have gone out and left the lights on. Why wouldn't you let me go into your apartment? What were you afraid I'd find?"

She regarded him coolly for a long time before she answered. "Me," she said. "I value my privacy. I don't want you or anybody else to have that."

"So you never let anyone in?"

"Who I let in or don't let in is my business. This is still America, isn't it?"

Her studied coolness amused him, but he kept a straight face. "Yes. No unreasonable search and seizure. Would it have been so unreasonable for me to ask questions in your kitchen while you put away your groceries?"

"It would have violated my privacy."

"Are you sure you didn't have another reason?"

She considered. "If I did," she said finally, "it had nothing to do with your case. My life is my own. I don't have to explain myself to anybody."

"That's true—but it sounds lonely." He expected her to shrug it off or take offense, but instead she was amused. Out of the blue, he asked, "What's your brother's name?"

"What?"

"Don't have an answer? Did you make up the story about the well?"

She shook her head. "My brother's name is Andrew. What does this have to do with anything?"

"Probably nothing, but I am curious. You didn't tell me where you grew up. You mentioned a well, so I'd guess somewhere rural?"

She sighed. "A small town in Idaho. You never

heard of it. Are we done?"

He was about to say they had barely started, but he saw Camille come off the elevator and thought better of it. Sariah's eyes followed his, and she got to her feet.

"Don't rush off," he said.

"What do you want from me?" she asked fretfully.

"The truth would be a good start."

"You have that."

Camille opened the door. "Am I interrupting something?" she asked, her voice dripping with sarcasm.

"I was just leaving," Sariah told her.

"You'd better be. I know the brother is a foxy dude, but you can't be winding him up on city time."

Sariah stared at her. "I'm sorry," she said. "I don't understand what you're saying."

"Do you speak English?" Camille asked, very sweetly for her.

"Yes. Do you?" Sariah asked with perfect politeness.

"Beat it, girl. We've got business."

Sariah gave Jesse an enigmatic look and left the room, giving Camille a wide berth.

"Honest to God," Camille said, closing the door behind her, although they usually left it open. "You and these slovenly white women. Apparently she's never heard of mascara."

"That's unkind," Jesse told her. "She's an unsophisticated small town girl, that's all."

"Oh, is that all?" She noticed the Java Prince change still lying on the desk and raised her eyebrows. "Taking donations?" she asked.

"Something like that." He shoved the bills and

coins into his pocket, offering no explanation.

"You have the DNA report?" Camille asked.

"Yes, and it backs up her description. I know you think she's blowing smoke, but she may be an eyewitness."

"If she is, she'd better say so. I got a copy of Capek's death certificate and a subpoena for the insurance records, which should settle that little matter."

"I hope so," Jesse agreed. "I wish I could get a search warrant for Brennan's apartment. She has to be hiding something."

"What? You can't talk your way into a lady's boudoir?"

"No, and wanting to protect her privacy isn't sufficient grounds. It's the reason search warrants were invented."

"That's very politically correct of you, but I'm sure you can charm your way in."

"Is that the effect I have on the female of the species?" Jesse asked.

Camille snorted. "Not on me, but you have your little ways."

"In this case, I think *you'd* have a better shot."

"At charm?"

"Or intimidation." He smiled to soften the remark, but she didn't respond anyway. She had other things on her mind.

"You want to go with me to the insurance office? I can't wait to inconvenience that little twerp."

"I wouldn't want to cramp your style. Let me see the death certificate. Maybe I'll talk to the doctor."

She handed him the document. "Good luck with

that," she said. He realized at once what she meant: the doctor's signature was practically illegible. "His name should be in the insurance records," she said. "I'll call you when I get them."

"I think it's Young," he decided. "I'll call the hospital." She nodded and headed off on her own errand.

According to the death certificate, Kazimir Capek had died at Holy Cross—a small, private Catholic hospital. Jesse called the number for administration. A gravelly male voice answered. "I'm trying to locate a doctor who was working at the hospital three years ago," Jesse told him. "I believe the last name is Young."

"Dr. Young is still here. Would you like me to transfer your call to her office?"

He wouldn't—it was often useful to talk to witnesses before they had time to prepare. "What is her first name, please?"

"Helen."

"Thank you." He hung up and studied the signature on the death certificate. The scrawled first name might conceivably be Helen. Would it be too much to ask for a doctor to write legibly on a legal document?

He didn't make it to Holy Cross after all. He would have preferred to continue making the Logan murder a top priority, but the first, intensive phase of the investigation, involving teams of officers and fruitless follow-up on dozens of leads, had ended, and it was essentially a cold case. All they had to suggest it might be worthwhile to pursue a dead suspect was the word of a single, probably unreliable, witness.

He spent the next three hours questioning Nicholas

Burns, a young patrolman whose partner had fired his gun in the line of duty. Nobody had been killed, but Homicide was responsible for investigating all officer-involved shootings resulting in injury. Burns was a competent, personable young man, but the exhaustively detailed interrogation required left them thoroughly sick of each other.

Jesse's interview notes were only a small part of the voluminous documentation of the incident, but he was confident it would be ruled a justified shooting. The suspect had been armed, an adult, and of the same race as the officer, so nothing was likely to spark community outrage.

He didn't see Dr. Young the next day either. The Thurston case was about to go to trial, and the DA wanted to review his planned testimony in the morning, before he got tied up in jury selection. Afterward Jesse was presented with one task after another that was more important than confirming the death of a man only a self-proclaimed psychic believed was still alive.

At four-thirty, Michelle put through a call from Sariah Brennan. "I have some information for you," she said. She sounded troubled. "I was going to call anyway, but…do you only investigate murders?"

"Yes, but if you have information about other cases, I can pass it on. Been having visions again, have you?"

"You can be very disrespectful sometimes," she said.

"I didn't mean to be," he said, although he was a little tired of the psychic shtick. "What do you have?"

"I found something—I don't want to come to your office." He glanced at Camille—undoubtedly the reason.

"I'll be glad to come by your place," he offered.

She didn't rise to the bait. "I'm at work now. I could meet you somewhere."

Jesse glanced at his watch. "What time do you get off?"

"Five o'clock."

"I'll pick you up at five."

"I don't think…all right. I have to go." She hung up.

Camille had heard enough to guess the rest. "Got a hot date?" she asked.

"Hardly," he said. Was it a date? Of course not, but it did feel more personal than it should.

His watch showed two minutes to five when he opened the door of World of Wings. It was quieter than the first time, the bird songs muted. He was immediately greeted by the shop owner: "We're closing, unless you're ready to buy a nice little canary?" She smiled at him. "Or did you come for another kind of bird?"

Sariah was near the back of the shop, covering bird cages, wearing what might be the same pink smock. She wasn't particularly happy to see him. "I can wait in the car," he suggested, and she nodded assent.

"I think a nice, cheerful songbird would be just the thing for you," the owner coaxed.

"Thank you," he said as he backed toward the door. "I'll think about it." He looked back at Sariah in time to catch a small smile of satisfaction.

He leaned against the car and waited, as he had in front of her apartment. It wasn't long before she came out. She had what he thought was a new purse, but otherwise looked the way she had then—pink-smocked and serious. She nodded curtly and got in the car, not waiting for him to open the door for her.

"Where to?" he asked.

She didn't answer and turned her gaze to the street.

"Java Prince?" he suggested.

"Yes, all right. Whatever. I have to give you something. I could have taken it to the police station, but...I guess I trust you. Are you trustworthy?" She looked at him, her eyes dark and grave.

"Very," he said and started the car.

"I do have something else about your case, but I don't know if it will help even if you believe me."

"New information never hurts," he said. "Let me decide what it's worth."

"The other victim's name is Elisabeth—with an s. He hasn't found her yet."

"How do you...yeah, okay. That's all you have?"

"I told you it wasn't much...a young woman, first name Elisabeth."

"So if we pulled up the driver's license pictures of every woman in Carroll City with that first name, you couldn't pick her out?"

"No, I never saw her, and I don't know if she lives here. I know it's not much help, but I didn't want her to be murdered because I didn't tell you. Now it's on you."

"Thanks," he said dryly.

"Maybe the Java Prince isn't such a good idea," she said. "Can you pull over somewhere?"

"I can." He took the next opportunity and drove into the parking lot of a supermarket.

Sariah opened her purse and took out an iPhone. "I

found this on the bus," she said. She looked up at him, clearly troubled. "I didn't see who left it. I was going to give it to the bus driver, you know, for the lost and found, but he was talking to another passenger, and I looked to see if I could tell who it belonged to. I…I don't know how to use it, and I guess I pushed the wrong button, or maybe it was…" She held it out to him. He reached across her to get a disposable glove and an evidence bag out of the glove compartment and took the phone carefully with two gloved fingers. He turned it on with the slightest touch. "Photos," she prompted.

He was still thinking this was something to do with Rosa Logan's murder, so the first image was totally unexpected. He stared at it, feeling a kind of chilling anger that made him understand how crimes of passion could be committed "in cold blood." It was child pornography of the ugliest kind. He glanced at Sariah. She was looking out the window and had a hand over her mouth. He touched the screen and scanned through several more images before he turned it off. It took him a minute to regain his voice. "You didn't see who left it?"

"No. I didn't notice anybody. I was reading a book most of the time, and when I got up, it was next to me, shoved back in the seat."

"And you don't get like psychic vibrations or something from it?"

He didn't think he had been disrespectful, but she said, "No," very stiffly. "Nice city you have here," she added.

"Unfortunately, things like this go on everywhere."

"If you say so."

"Thank you," he said. "I'll give it to the sex crimes investigators."

"That doesn't deserve to be called sex," she said.

"I suppose not. This is an expensive phone, not a prepaid disposable, so they should be able to find out who owned it. What bus was it? The surveillance camera might show who had it."

"The number ten—the one that gets to Obama Street about eight."

"So you've had this all day?"

"Yes. I didn't know what to do. My fingerprints are on it—will they have to—?"

"Take your prints to exclude them? Why, is that a problem?"

She didn't answer. She was looking out the window again.

"Ms. Brennan…"

"Sariah," she said, her eyes still on the street.

"Sariah, are your prints in the system?"

"I don't know. I don't think so. Why would they be?"

"If you've ever been arrested or worked for the government—or they might have been found at the scene of a crime. Is that what you're afraid of?"

She looked at him. "No, of course not. If they need me to come in and be fingerprinted, I will, but I'd rather not have anything more to do with…*that*. I can get a bus from here."

"Don't be silly. I'll take you home. Thank you for giving me this—it might help to catch a very bad dude." He started the car.

"You can drop me at the corner," she said. "I'd rather Peggy didn't see me come home in a police car."

"It's unmarked," he pointed out.

"Everybody knows what it is," she said. Her tone held something very like pity.

"I can't figure you out," he confessed. "Small town girl? Street smart?" *Psychic? Liar?*

"I can't figure you out either." She pointed to the Java Prince ahead on the right, and he pulled over.

"As long as we're here, can I buy you a cup of coffee or something?"

"Why?"

He shrugged. "I guess to thank you for…"

"Doing my civic duty? I just wanted to get rid of it."

"Maybe we could try to figure each other out."

"That doesn't sound appropriate," she said.

"No, it isn't, but…." Something in her expression made him think it wouldn't be a mistake to pursue this, but he wasn't sure what his motives were. "Would you rather not be seen with me? This is your neighborhood, after all."

"What do you mean?" She sounded genuinely puzzled. "Because you're a cop?"

"Yes, or…you know, the race thing."

She didn't know whether to be shocked or amused. "Well," was all she could think of to say and then, looking away, "I think you're very attractive." When she finally met his eyes, she added, "I'm sorry, is that all right to say? I didn't mean to embarrass you."

"You didn't. I think you're attractive too."

"Not really," she said dismissively. "I know I'm not what you're used to. You want something from me, but I'm not sure what."

"Neither am I," he said with perfect honesty.

"Maybe a cup of coffee would help us sort it out."

"Coffee keeps me awake." The refusal sounded final, but she didn't get out of the car.

"You could have tea or decaf," he suggested.

She studied him. "If I have coffee with you, will you buy a bird from World of Wings?"

He laughed, and she gave him a slow, warming smile in return. "I think it would have to be at least dinner if I did," he said.

"Not tonight. One cup of coffee, and then I want to walk home and take a very long, hot shower and see if I can forget those pictures ever existed."

"Sounds good to me."

She settled on a decaf vanilla latte, and he ordered his usual French roast. The Java Prince was less busy than it had been the first time, and they had a choice of tables. "Can we sit by the window?" she asked, and he followed her and pulled out her chair with his free hand, wondering why it was so awkward.

"Thank you," she said, smiling.

"So you came from a small town in Idaho?" he asked. He might as well have asked for her sign.

"Yes. You would like it—or maybe you would find it boring. It's very peaceful, no crime to speak of."

"No law enforcement job opportunities?"

"We do have cops. And they drive Interceptors."

"I see. I don't think you told me the name of the town."

"Mackay…I knew you wouldn't have heard of it."

"Mackay? No."

"It was named after a Scottish anarchist, John Henry Mackay."

"Odd choice. Are you an anarchist?"

"No, but I think people should be able to lead their own lives."

"I'm all for that."

"Where did you grow up?" she asked.

"I was born in San Francisco, but I've lived here most of my adult life."

"So you like it?"

"I do. Not much weather, but pretty laid back. It also has a better-funded police department than San Francisco. It doesn't hurt having a former chief of police as our mayor."

"I'm still getting used to living in a city."

"How long have you been here?"

"Less than a year. Why did you decide to become a cop?"

"Rocket science requires too many years of school, and I wasn't good at anything else."

"That's not a real answer."

"It will have to do."

That was the extent of the information exchanged, but Sariah found the situation more amusing than uncomfortable. She asked a few questions about police work, but didn't show much interest in the answers. He was used to dealing with all kinds of people and thought he was pretty good at interrogating suspects, but he hadn't had this much trouble talking to a woman since junior high school.

"Why is an attractive woman like you living alone?" he asked.

"Same reason you are," she said. She gave him a warm, straightforward smile, and her face was transformed.

"What?" he asked.

"You're trying so hard," she said.

"Is that bad?"

"Do you think if you flirt with me I'll tell you all my secrets?"

"Will you?"

"I did—I mean everything relating to your case."

"That's your story, and you're sticking to it?"

"Yes. Take it or leave it. Thanks for the coffee." She was relaxed, smiling, amused, and as she got up she briefly put her hand on his. The gesture was almost patronizing, but when their hands touched he felt something he hadn't when they shook hands the first day.

Later, in the middle of the night, he was able to convince himself he was just intrigued by the mystery. What was she up to? Why give him information and hold back anything really useful? How *did* she know about the teeth marks? What was the "misunderstanding" at Maxine's? How could she know about another potential victim? Was something happening between them? When she asked him to call her Sariah, did she guess how easily he already thought of her that way?

Chapter Five

"How was your date?" Camille asked first thing next morning.

"Don't start," Jesse warned. "I'm not in the mood."

"Struck out?"

"I met with an informant," he said, enunciating very carefully, "who gave me pictures of a little girl being raped."

Camille sobered. "Killed?"

"Not as far as I know. I gave them to Vince."

"Anything identifiable?"

"Maybe. We'll see." He hoped Sex Crimes would find the owner of the phone or the other fingerprints on it would match a likely suspect, so Sariah wouldn't have to come in—and regret giving it to him.

He did make a halfhearted effort to identify "Elisabeth." He checked DMV records for women with that name who lived anywhere near Rosa Logan's apartment, the crime scene, or the house on Vista Road. He also examined, not for the first time, the record for Sariah's California ID card, which told him nothing more enlightening than that she was twenty-six years old and a registered organ donor.

Idaho—DMV, Tax Commission, Vital Records— had proved to have nothing under her name at all. Like Rosa Logan, she seemed not to have existed until she surfaced in Carroll City very recently.

He still hadn't made it to the hospital to see Dr. Young, but Camille's diligent review of the insurance records had turned up nothing suspicious. In the spirit of dotting the i's and crossing the t's, he headed to Holy Cross.

Dr. Helen Young was in her thirties, a white woman with black hair, probably very pretty when she wasn't frazzled and impatient. She told him she didn't have time for him and he should make an appointment. Undaunted, Jesse showed her the picture of Kazimir Capek. "Does he look familiar?"

With a resigned sigh, she settled the Ben Franklin-style glasses suspended from a chain around her neck on her perfect nose. "No. I don't remember everybody I've seen in the last three years. Do you? Now, if you'll—"

"Just one more minute, I promise." He showed her the death certificate. "Do you remember signing this?"

"No. If you'll come back in an hour or so, I'll check my records to see if I did see this patient, but I'm busy right now." She started away, but turned back to say, "It's not my signature."

Two hours later he was still sitting in Dr. Young's office, waiting for her to check her records. The time wasn't completely wasted; he made several calls, which didn't result in any real progress but at least wouldn't have to be made later. It started raining while he waited, and the spatter of drops against the window reminded him of the first time he had seen Sariah. She was nothing more than a reasonably pretty young white woman, completely unknown to him. He wasn't sure he knew her any better now, but something disturbed him about the memory of the casual parting at the Java

Prince—Sariah's smile, the touch of her hand, her hair falling softly around her face.

When Dr. Young finally came in, she was calmer, but still very brisk. She took the death certificate, read through it quickly, and turned to a filing cabinet. "You'll have to check with Medical Records to see if he was admitted, but I can at least tell you if I—nope, no Capek."

"Would you mind looking at the picture again? Anything ring a bell? The scar maybe?"

She studied it for about two seconds. "No. The cause of death was cardiovascular disease? Do you have any idea how common that is? It's the leading cause of death worldwide."

"But at fifty-two?"

"More common than you might imagine. Lifestyle is a major factor. Mr. Capek—let's just say he doesn't strike me as a vegetarian. I would guess he had high blood pressure and it wasn't controlled with medication. Look at his complexion—very unhealthy—and this vein!"

"Okay," he said. "I guess that's why you have the M.D. after your name."

She looked at him over her reading glasses, the first time she really seemed to *see* him. "That's right," she said, as if she suspected he was mocking her. "Think about it the next time you cut into a juicy steak. Are you aware that African-American men have one of the highest hypertension rates in the world? When was the last time you had your blood pressure checked?"

"I'm not sure, but I think it's probably higher than usual right now. You said this wasn't your signature— what makes you so sure?"

She gave him another look over her glasses. "I think I would know," she said, but her voice was softer. She took a folder from the cabinet and selected a sheet from it. "*This* is my signature," she said. It was a lot more legible than the one on the death certificate.

"Do you have any idea whose signature it is? I'm almost sure this is a Y—wouldn't you say? The insurance company read it that way too."

"Yes," she agreed. "I think it could be Young—I can understand the mistake, but it isn't my signature. Check with Medical Records; I'm sure they can straighten this out."

"Is there another Dr. Young at Holy Cross? Or was there three years ago?"

"Nope. Just me." She smiled, but he could see she was ready for him to leave.

Jesse showed her the death certificate again. "Would your signature be different if you were in a hurry? Or could it have changed in the last three years?"

"I'm always in a hurry, and I haven't changed it."

"Would you remember? I wouldn't." He softened the interrogatory tone with a smile. Was he flirting with her? Did he do that? Flirt with women to get information?

Dr. Young shrugged. She went back to the files, checked several pages, and handed him two. The dates were about three years ago, and the signatures were both similar to the first one she had shown him. If anything they were even less like the hasty scrawl on the death certificate. The Y was particularly distinctive. "Check with Medical Records," she said again. "Even though he's dead, you'll have to put your request in writing—I'm sure you know the rules. And have your blood pressure checked."

****

He arrived at World of Wings about half an hour before closing time. Sariah was busy with a customer, and he stood near the door and watched her work. She wasn't as pretty as Dr. Young, who had beautiful hair and knew how to apply makeup, but something about her caught the eye. His eye anyway. She looked tired—she had been on her feet all day.

She spotted him before she was finished with her customer and was apparently a little unnerved. He—or maybe cops in general—had that effect on some people, but she should be used to him by now. Was she concerned about something in particular?

He pretended to be interested in a display of bird harnesses—he hadn't known such a thing existed—until she came to join him. "I didn't expect to see you today," she said.

"Me either, but we should talk about a few things, and I thought maybe over dinner…?"

She had to think about it, and then she said, "That means you're going to buy a bird?"

"Oh—uh—I'm not in the market for a pet."

"Then why do you keep coming to a pet shop? You said it would have to be dinner—"

He glanced around the room. "Where's the boss?"

"She left early. I have to lock up."

"She trusts you."

"I wish you did. Men usually prefer larger birds—more macho, I guess. How about an African Grey Parrot? They're very intelligent and long-lived. Do you have a large apartment?"

"You're kidding…aren't you?"

She laughed. "Yes. It's better to start with a small bird—lovebirds are fairly quiet, or… Oh, I know." She led him toward the back of the shop and opened a cage. "This is a European goldfinch," she said. "Isn't he gorgeous?" The bird was gray, black, white, and yellow, with a red face. "Not as flashy as a Macaw," she acknowledged, "but a lot less trouble."

"It's very nice," he said, "but…"

"Of course you'll need a cage and a cover and a supply of Finch Blend and a water bowl."

"Sariah…your boss said you weren't a bad saleswoman, but I didn't come in here to buy a bird."

"But you will," she said.

He did. It wasn't cheap, either. When it was all added up, it came to more than three hundred dollars.

"I guess cops don't make a lot of money," Sariah said apologetically as she rang it up.

"I couldn't lavish you with diamonds, but I can't complain."

"I'm not a diamonds kind of girl," she said. "They say enough is as good as a feast."

"Yes, but what is enough?"

"That's a very good question. Now that I've made you spend all this money, you don't have to take me to dinner." She began to close up, and he had to follow her around to continue the conversation.

"Dinner was part of the deal," he said.

"I'd have to go home and change," she said, gesturing to her pink smock.

"That can be arranged."

"What are you going to name him?"

"Who?"

She laughed. "The bird."

"I have no idea."

"Did you have pets when you were a kid?"

"A hamster once. We had a dog, but he never liked me."

"What's not to like? Did you make fun of him?"

"I'm sorry if it seemed like I was making fun of you, Sariah."

The bell above the front door dinged as someone came in. She had covered about half of the cages, quieting the occupants, or they might not have heard it. The young man who came in looked a bit scruffy to Jesse, and he kept an eye on him. He bought a four-pound bag of parrot food and wasn't inside long, but it made Jesse think like a cop.

"Are you alone here a lot?" he asked.

"Now and then."

"Well, be careful."

"I'm always careful."

When the shop was secured, they put the goldfinch cage in the back seat of his car. "Strangest suspect I've ever had in here," he said.

As they drove toward Vista Road, Sariah asked, "Will you get in trouble for taking somebody involved in a case to dinner?"

"No, I'll tell them you started it."

"I didn't—"

"At the Java Prince the first time, you asked if I was married."

"I wasn't checking your marital status; I was trying to get you to go home and leave me alone."

"Look," he said, feeling very unsure of his ground. "Nothing is going to happen. I know things seem to be moving kind of fast, but..." He started to sweat and wished he had kept his mouth shut.

"I don't need to shave my legs?"

He risked a quick glance at her. "Are you making fun of me now?" he asked.

"We'll only be discussing the case, right? But I need to know where we're going. I need to know what to wear, and I want to tell Peggy where you're taking me in case I end up murdered. Yes, I'm making fun of you."

"Okay," he said. "As long as I know. Do you like Mexican food? I thought maybe Quique's—it's casual, so jeans or a skirt would be fine."

"You're wearing a suit."

"I'll take off my tie."

"A skirt, then."

She didn't ask him to park down the street this time, and he pulled into the driveway at 4763 Vista Road. "I'll be five minutes," she promised as she got out of the car. Jesse thought she might have asked him up to wait, under the circumstances, but it didn't seem to have occurred to her.

"Why did I buy the damn bird?" he asked aloud in the silent car. As an excuse to keep in touch with her? A customer had a right to return for advice or supplies. To what purpose? To find out what she knew?

He didn't time her, but he was pretty sure it was more than five minutes. She was a woman, after all. She had made a very appropriate choice—a full, dark skirt and an embroidered blouse—long-sleeved and not a Mexican design, or she would have resembled the waitresses at Quique's. She also wore more makeup than she usually did—she *had* heard of mascara.

"You look very pretty," he said.

"Thank you, Jesse. I guess I can call you Jesse now, right?"

"Yes. Detective Aaron would be a bit formal for Quique's. Will the bird be all right in the car, or should I stop at my apartment and leave him?"

"I won't go to your apartment. I mean it wouldn't be appropriate. I'll wait in the car."

"Trust works both ways," he said.

"I didn't say I didn't trust you."

"Do you?"

She laughed. "No. Are you allowed to drive this car on your personal time—or is it not personal if we discuss the case?"

"Actually, this is my own car. The department has a program so detectives can buy the Interceptors at a discount. Or I could drive my own and get a gas allowance, like Camille."

"So you *chose* to look like a cop all the time?"

"It's a good car," he said. He supposed she was laughing at him again. The evening promised to be interesting, one way or another.

Chapter Six

Quique's was a white adobe hacienda-style house with a red tiled roof and a central patio where colorful umbrellas shaded the tables. Jesse preferred dining al fresco, but it would be too cold tonight for Sariah's cotton blouse. The rain had stopped, but it was still overcast and windy. Inside it was noisier and a little less atmospheric, but this was *not* a romantic rendezvous. More like a business dinner, if not a formal interrogation.

A waitress in an off-the-shoulder Mexican blouse showed them to a table and asked what they would like to drink. Sariah turned to Jesse for a recommendation. Quique's was famous for its margaritas, but he suggested one of their virgin fruit drinks, and he ordered coffee.

"You do drink a lot of coffee," she said. She directed her attention to the menu with its colorful pictures and lavish descriptions. "What looks good? Everything. So many choices…"

"I hope you like Mexican food. You didn't say."

"I have no idea. I don't think Taco Bell counts." She shook her head in amazement. "It all sounds wonderful. Coconut shrimp with mango chipotle sauce. What *is* chipotle?"

"Chili pepper, but it's not too hot."

"I'll have that," she said decisively.

They were ready to order when the waitress brought the drinks. Jesse was used to independent women who ordered for themselves, but Sariah seemed to expect him to do it. He ordered the shrimp for her and a Mexican chopped salad.

"A salad?" she asked when the waitress was gone.

It was the perfect opening. "Today a doctor told me I should watch my blood pressure."

"Oh!" She looked concerned.

"Guess who?"

"What do you mean?"

"Dr. Helen Young. Her name is on your suspect's death certificate."

"Except he's not dead." Sariah took a sip of her drink and studied him gravely.

"He might not be," he said cautiously.

"Really?"

"Dr. Young says it's not her signature. The admission records show she was the doctor of record. He came into the emergency room three years ago with chest pains and was admitted to rule out a heart attack. Angina was the initial diagnosis. The rest of the records are missing. Dr. Young doesn't remember him. She does remember being on vacation when the insurance records show they checked with the hospital to confirm the information on the death certificate."

"Which means…?"

"Maybe nothing, but they didn't talk to Dr. Young. It's usual to confirm with the person who signed the certificate, but someone on the staff may have given them enough information to satisfy them."

"Did you talk to his wife?"

"Detective Farris is planning to, but so far she's

been hard to find. The address the insurance company has is out of date, and yet somebody has been cashing the checks, at a different place each time—grocery stores, Money Marts, never banks."

"I told you he wasn't dead." She was calm but triumphant.

"Maybe—but we have nowhere to start to find him. His wife sold his car, and there isn't one registered to her. None of Rosa Logan's acquaintances recognize him." He leaned forward and spoke more urgently. "Sariah, we can't play this game anymore. If he is alive, I have to know how you knew. You know more than you've told me. Do you know him? Were you there?"

"I told you I wasn't. Are you calling me a liar?"

Jesse took a deep breath and sipped his coffee. "You *are* a liar," he said.

"You got me dressed up and took me out to dinner to tell me that?"

"I took you out to dinner because…no, I don't have an answer. If you think I'm in control in this situation, you're wrong. I don't know why I care, but I do, and you lied to me. You didn't find the cell phone on the number ten bus to Obama Street."

She was more than surprised. Her cheeks flushed, and she lowered her gaze. He let her take it in and waited for her answer. "How do you know?" she asked, and then she looked up and tried to brazen it out. "I mean what makes you think so? What difference does it make where I got it?"

"The sex crimes investigators have the security tape from the bus. Two people sat next to you. One was a teenage girl. She had a cell phone. She was texting. She was still texting when she got off the bus. No big deal; the phone could have been in the seat before you got on, and you didn't happen to notice it. Or the other person might have had it, and it was never visible to the camera. But you didn't take it up to the bus driver. You didn't have it in your hand when you got off. You were reading your book until just before the bus stopped, and you got right up and got off."

"That's not how I remember it," she said. "Maybe…they looked at the wrong date."

"We're not amateurs, Sariah, and we don't like to be messed with. I appreciate your turning it in, but we have to know where it's been."

"Were there fingerprints?" she asked. "Or you said they could find out who owned it?"

"That's not the point. Do *you* know who owns it?"

"No, of course not. I would have told you."

"It belongs to a woman named Kimberly Jackson. No, forget I told you her name. I shouldn't have. What are you hiding? Who are you trying to protect?"

She shook her head. "Myself?" she suggested.

"Talk to me," he urged. "I can't work in the dark."

"Did they find Kim—the woman whose name I never heard?"

"Yes. She has a seven-year-old daughter."

"Oh, God. Seven?"

"No, she's not the girl in the pictures—not yet. The mother has no idea who could have taken them. It could be a man in her life, someone she trusts with her daughter. It could be somebody she hasn't even met. She says the phone was stolen."

"Don't they always say that?"

"They?"

"People whose possessions—cars, guns, phones—

are connected to a crime."

"You mean on TV? What have you been watching?"

"I'm sorry; I know it's not a realistic picture of police work."

"That's what you're sorry for?"

The waitress came back to the table with plates laden with enticing food. "Careful, it's hot," she told Sariah. "Anything else I can get you?" she asked. "More coffee, sir?"

"Nothing, thank you," Jesse told her.

Sariah tried a little of her rice, cut a piece of shrimp, and tasted it before she met his eyes. "This is very good," she said. "How's your salad?"

"Is that all you have to say?"

"The shrimp is very crisp," she said guilelessly. "Does Taco Bell even have shrimp?"

Jesse shook his head. "I'll tell you, I've dealt with a lot of witnesses. Some were reluctant. Some were overeager and made things up. Some lied to me. Some were mistaken. But I've never met one quite like you."

"Did you take any of them out to dinner?"

"No. Come on, give me a break. I bought a damned European goldfinch for you."

"*Carduelis carduelis*," she said. "You'll thank me in the long run. He will light up your life."

"It doesn't need to be lit up. Tell me the truth."

"I was mistaken," she said. "Maybe it wasn't yesterday."

"And you kept the phone for days? Do you want them to get the security tapes for the last week? Is that the way you want to go? Detective Farris was right, you know; it is a crime to give false information to the police. It *is* obstruction of justice."

"I did find it on the bus yesterday. I put it in my purse. I never tried to give it to the bus driver or find out who owned it."

"So you looked at the pictures while you were still sitting on the bus?"

"Yes," she said, but her hesitation told him it was another lie. "What about the other person who sat next to me? Could they identify him?"

"Not so far. Do you remember it being a man?"

"I don't think I noticed at all. Was it?"

"Yes. Tall, African-American, about fifty," he said. "Do you remember seeing him?"

"No. The man in the pictures was white."

"Yes. But the man on the bus could have taken the pictures or known who did or bought them from somebody else—possession is a crime too. He would have to be pretty stupid to have them on his phone and be so careless with it. A pro would have had it password protected. We need to find him, but we don't want to waste time searching for him if he never had it. Are you going to help?"

"I don't know who had it. I wanted to give it to you, not the bus driver, because…I wanted to see you again."

"You are so full of shit," he said.

"Well, I did." It sounded true. Was it? She blushed a little. It was very attractive.

"The trouble with telling lies is sometimes it's hard to tell when you stop."

"I was embarrassed, that's all."

"Bullshit. Nothing embarrasses you…Almost nothing." He remembered her pretty blush. Was she ashamed of the lies, or of her feelings? Or chagrined because he'd caught her?

"Why aren't the sex crimes investigators asking me these questions?" she asked.

"They will. Are you going to give them a different story?"

"Don't worry. I won't tell them you were inappropriate with me."

"Was that a threat? Shit, Sariah—"

"I wish you wouldn't use that kind of language."

"Well, excuse the hell out of me!" He took a deep breath and tried to calm down. He picked at his salad—the chicken was tender, but it might as well have been cardboard.

"I'm sorry," she said.

"For...?"

"Making things hard for you when I was trying to help."

"I thought maybe you enjoyed it—making things hard."

"No, and I didn't mean to raise your blood pressure."

"My blood pressure is fine. Let me ask you this one more time: How did you know Kazimir Capek was alive?"

"Capek? That's his name?"

"I shouldn't have told you that."

"K.C.," she said. "Casey." She was pleased, and he would be in deep shit if Camille found out.

"How did you know he was alive?" he repeated.

"I told you."

"Yeah, okay. We're not done with this, but let's shelve it for tonight."

"In the interest of your blood pressure?"

"If you like." He took a sip of coffee and tried again to enjoy the salad, piled high with chunks of fresh avocado and tomato.

"It's nice here," Sariah said, unruffled.

"Even better outside on a sunny day," he said. "You never tried real Mexican food before? No local cantina in Mackay? Rubio's? Baja Fresh?"

She shook her head. "But you've probably never had homemade chili and cornbread or thick-cut Idaho fries. Real Mackay comfort food—barbecued ribs, macaroni and cheese, banana pudding…"

"Ribs, yes, but it's been a long time for me and home cooking. Do you cook?"

"Yes, or I used to. Now…I work long hours, and I have a microwave."

He detected a barb in the last phrase—she remembered him asking at the Java Prince. He still didn't understand why it annoyed her.

"What about your family?" she asked. "Do you go home for Thanksgiving or Christmas, eat your mother's cooking?"

"If nobody gets murdered. It's been three years now."

"Traditional roast turkey and trimmings?"

"Sage stuffing, whole cranberries, followed by my grandmother's sweet potato pie…"

Sariah smiled. "Why is it so much fun to talk about food?" she asked.

The rest of the meal was pleasant enough, but Jesse couldn't forget what simmered underneath—anger, but not just that, more than that.

On the ride back to Vista Road, silence prevailed.

He didn't know what she was thinking about. He didn't even know what he was thinking about. Lights were on behind the closed curtains of the house. He parked short of the driveway, where the nearest streetlight filled the front seat with a dim glow.

"Thank you," she said. "I enjoyed it, and I appreciate you keeping me up to date on the investigation."

"Is that what I was doing?"

She gave him an enigmatic smile. She had said she found him attractive, but as a kind of conventional compliment. He wondered if she could be as attracted to him as he was to her. He thought yes, but there would be hell to pay if he was wrong—and even if he was right. She was a witness, a lying, maddening witness, and it was unprofessional to think of her in any other way, but something *was* happening between them. He studied the sensitive curve of her slightly parted lips. She had retouched her lipstick in Quique's restroom, a bare hint of color.

He kissed her. Her mouth surprised him, soft and sweet and willing, almost hungry, but with something held back. She was scared, but she wanted this. They were not investigator and witness; they were two people trying to find their way to—what? He didn't know.

She didn't say anything afterward, which was unnerving. "I guess I shouldn't have done that," he said.

"Because of the case," she said, almost but not quite a question.

"What if there wasn't a case?" She didn't answer, and he couldn't read her expression. She made no effort to get out of the car. "Can I come up?" he asked.

"No," she said at once, the old stubborn note in her

voice, but she softened it with, "It's a little fast for me."

Caution did seem advisable, and he got out and went around to open the door for her. She smiled her appreciation of the courtesy. "Keep in touch," he said.

"I will," she said. "Take good care of *Carduelis carduelis*."

Jesse watched her climb the stairs and disappear inside before he got back in the car. He sat in the semi-darkness for another minute, remembering the kiss, and all he could feel was a lingering sense of discovery. "Damn," he said aloud and started the car.

Chapter Seven

The bird wasn't much trouble, but he was a constant reminder that Jesse had been conned into an unwise entanglement in an already complicated case. Because Sariah had twice referred to the cheery little finch by the Latin name *Carduelis carduelis,* he dubbed him C.C., which could also stand for his adopted city. He hoped she would approve of his choice and wanted to tell her—and no, he would not find an excuse to talk to her. When they got to the bottom of the insurance snafu and found Kazimir Capek—alive or dead—would be soon enough.

He was unable to find the slightest hint of a leak in the department—nobody in Forensics or Records who appeared to recognize Sariah's name or face or touch anywhere on the fringes of her life. She had never been arrested or filed a complaint or witness statement before. He even confirmed that the clerks who took the bus to work never took the number ten. He was stymied—in everything relating to her, he was completely confounded.

His next encounter with her was unexpected, in the elevator of CCPD headquarters on Friday morning. The day was cool and cloudy, and she wore an unbuttoned coat over the familiar pink smock, with her hands in the pockets. She wasn't as surprised as he was, and he asked, "Were you coming to see me?"

"No, I'm not stalking you," she said with a laugh. He pressed the button for the main floor.

"What are you doing here?" he asked, trying to sound simply curious and not downright rude.

"I had to talk to the Sex Crimes investigators," she explained. "They don't think I'm such a suspicious character."

"Did you tell them the same story you told me?"

"I told them what I knew, and they told me you *asked* to see the security tapes. I thought they shared them with you because you gave them the phone, but it's a completely separate investigation. You weren't supposed to tell me the woman's name because you weren't supposed to know it. You were checking up on me."

"Yeah, we do that when we think a witness might be lying to us."

"There's no *us*—bad cop doesn't know what you're doing, does she?"

"You mean that I took you out to dinner?"

"Among other things." A memory of that single, surprising kiss surfaced unbidden as the elevator door opened onto the busy lobby.

He was afraid she was about to give him the slip again and said, "We should talk. Where are you headed?"

"I have to get back to work."

"I'll give you a ride."

"I can take the bus."

"I'll give you a ride," he repeated and took her arm to steer her toward the door that led to the garage.

"Don't," she said. She didn't budge.

"Sorry." He let go of her arm. "Nice coat." The

69

style was simple, even plain, but the fabric had been soft and rich under his fingers. She didn't seem like somebody who would spend a lot on clothes, but maybe she had lived a more affluent lifestyle back in Mackay, Idaho. This could be a remnant of those days.

"Thank you," she said politely. She didn't agree to anything, but she did walk toward the door beside him.

"Are you really angry with me?" he asked. "I thought we parted friends at least."

"You were raising your blood pressure because I fudged a few details," she said. "This is why it doesn't work to mix work with pleasure."

"*Was* it pleasure?"

"Yes, but I don't think it should happen again, do you?"

"I don't know what I want to do, much less what I should do."

"You're kind of a mess, aren't you?" She was laughing at him, but she followed him into the garage and waited for him to open the car door for her.

Jesse kept away from more dangerous subjects on the drive to World of Wings and instead told her about C.C. He was right; she liked the name. By the time they arrived, she was in a relaxed enough mood to touch his hand before she got out of the car. "Thank you for the ride," she said.

Encouraged, he said, "I'll call you," and she didn't object.

Chapter Eight

Jesse didn't call Sariah. Instead he went to pick her up after work the following Wednesday to tell her a piece of good news. She was glad to see him, accepted the offer of a ride, and smiled in a way he found very encouraging. "Can I take you out to dinner?" he asked. "Quique's has a lot more on the menu to try, or we could go somewhere else if you'd rather."

"I don't feel like going out," she said, "but we do need to talk." That sounded promising on several levels. She sounded uncertain—but maybe she was just tired.

"We could pick up takeout and go to your place," he suggested. "Do you like Chinese?"

"I don't think that's a good idea."

"Chinese?"

"My place," she said. "I told you before…"

"What are you trying to hide?" he asked.

"It's not about having something to hide. It's about being me."

"I'm sorry, but it doesn't make any sense to me. What am I missing?"

"Does it bother you so much that I don't want you to see my crummy apartment?"

"Yes, it does bother me…" *Secrets. Lies.*

"I don't want to have to explain myself to anybody."

"What do you mean? You think I'll laugh at your

interior decorating choices?" She looked very stubborn, so he gave up. "Okay, okay, do you want to go to my place? Maybe order a pizza? We can talk...plus you can say hello to C.C."

"All right," she said. "But stop at Peggy's first, so I can change."

He tried again after he started the car. "Is it because I'm a cop? Or do I scare you in some other way?"

"It's not you," she said. "It's me."

"That sounds familiar."

"It's not as if I've invited every other man I know to come home with me and excluded you. I don't want to share that part of me with *anyone*. I like you, and yes, I'm very attracted to you, but we don't even know each other yet. I don't know what you want from me."

"Nothing you don't want to give. I want—I might want you in my life. Is that so hard to understand?"

"No, it's not, and I might want you in mine, but I don't want you *in* my life, walking all over my life, telling me what to do. I'm done with that."

"Okay, so somebody before was too controlling— you want to tell me who?" He had in mind an opportunity to punch somebody in the nose—with any luck the dude would still be stalking her, and he could be the hero of this piece.

"Everybody," she said. "Family, friends—just everybody. In a place like Mackay, everybody knows your business."

"All right," he said. Not as exciting as punching somebody, but a difficulty he could overcome. She was skittish, but she would come around. He didn't want to pursue the discussion to the point where they would both be out of the mood—if she was ever in the mood in the first place. Maybe he had misunderstood.

He parked half across the Dunwoods' driveway; Sariah didn't seem to care if she was seen in the Interceptor anymore. Had she told Peggy about dinner? She was back in record time, in black jeans and a lime green sweater, her hair brushed, her lipstick freshened.

"You look very nice," he said. "I mean you always do, but I appreciate the effort."

"It's not all for you," she said with a smile. "C.C. likes this color."

The first few minutes were easy. She surveyed the living room with interest and approval, commented on the flat-screen TV and the muted color scheme, and greeted C.C. like the old friend he was. She opened the cage, and C.C. tilted his head in alert inquiry. "Good," she said, "You're keeping the cage clean. It's a lot harder if you let it go." C.C. hopped toward her, and she touched his feathered head with a gentle finger. "Pretty bird," she said in the tone some women used to babies, and C.C. responded with two clear, musical notes.

When she was finished fussing over the goldfinch, Jesse gestured toward the couch. "So what do you think? Pizza? I think I have tomatoes and a cucumber— I could make a salad."

"I'm not hungry yet." She sat on the couch and glanced around again. "Very nice," she said. She patted one of the decorative pillows Erika had bought. "And you live here alone? Since your last girlfriend took the dog?"

"Except for C.C., of course."

"It's great, isn't it? Living alone? Eat when you want to eat, watch what you want to watch. Read, play music, whatever. Complete privacy. It can be hard to give up." Was this an apology for her earlier stubbornness?

"It can be lonely, though," he said. "Speaking of music, would you like me to put some on?"

"Yes, why not? What kind of music do you like?"

"A little of everything. I have mostly jazz here. How about you?"

"I listen to country and classical," she said. "Jazz would be fine." He went to the CD rack. What would she like? Had she agreed as she had to the coffee—when in Rome? He put on an album of standards by the Brad Mehldau Trio.

"C.C. likes this one," he said, and Sariah laughed. He sat down next to her. He hoped he wasn't close enough to make her uncomfortable, but he was drawn to her, to the intangible mystery that promised and eluded, and yes, to the scent of her skin and hair.

"I like the piano," she said politely. Without premeditation, he leaned in and kissed her. She didn't hold anything back this time.

"Do you do this a lot?" she asked. "I mean…with witnesses?"

"Never."

"It *is* inappropriate."

"I know it is," he agreed and did it again.

"You said you had something to tell me," Sariah reminded him.

"Yes. Vince in Sex Crimes…they made an arrest. The phone *was* stolen, but not before the owner's nephew borrowed it. So far he's charged with possession of child pornography, but he may cop to more, or lead them to other suspects."

"Then we can be done with it? I didn't like being anywhere near it."

"Out of our hands. Now if we could find Kazimir Capek or the mysterious Elisabeth…" He kissed her again and touched her fine, straight hair and the smooth curve of her jaw. "Was there something else you wanted to talk about? You said—"

"Where's the bedroom?" she asked. Jesse didn't know what to think, but his heart beat a little faster. He pointed in the general direction, and she looked, but didn't get up. Instead she pulled her sweater off, mussing her hair. She wasn't wearing a bra but what he thought was called a camisole. The sweater had tugged it free of the waistband of her jeans, baring her midriff, and the silky fabric was taut against her breasts. The desire to touch was very strong, but he kissed her again instead. Sariah shook her head with something like impatience, pulled the undergarment off, and ran her fingers through her tangled hair.

Her breasts were beautiful, firm and rounded, but his main impression was of their unnatural paleness, like unripe fruit. She wasn't the first white woman he had seen topless, but she was not a movie actress made up for the camera, and maybe Mackay, Idaho didn't have nude sunbathing or tanning beds. He took her breasts in his hands, and they did not feel unripe at all. Her skin was very warm and wonderfully soft.

He kissed her again, breathless and lightheaded. His thumbs stroked her nipples, and she arched her back and half reclined against the pillow behind her. He kissed her mouth again and pressed his lips against the hollow at the base of her throat. Her arms were around his neck, and he could feel her heartbeat under his hands.

The doorbell rang. Jesse took a deep breath. "Do you have to get it?" Sariah asked, her voice low and husky.

"No," he said, unnerved but in no way inclined to stop.

"Aaron!" The voice was unmistakable: Camille.

"Shit." He let go of Sariah. She put a finger to her lips, grabbed her sweater and camisole, and stood up. He thought she might be amused—at least she didn't appear to be angry. "Give me a minute," he said. She went into the bedroom and closed the door. Jesse straightened his clothes, switched off the stereo, and went to let Camille in. "What's up?" he asked.

She didn't wait on formalities; she barged right in. "I knew you would want to see this," she said as she handed him a folder. It contained a fax cover sheet and two documents: a high school transcript in the name of Rosanna Milne and a police report headed with the same name. He didn't have to read the report to get the gist—attached to it was a photograph of a young woman with a black eye and a split lip. She looked about eighteen, but she bore an uncanny resemblance to Rosa Logan. He turned back to the cover sheet—it was from the Lyon County, Nevada Sheriff's Office. It was the first lead to the real identity of their murder victim. He started to read the police report, a four-year-old assault complaint, but Camille interrupted. "Seriously?" she said. "You've got to be kidding me!"

"What?" He looked up at her. She was standing in the middle of the living room with her arms folded. She gave him a very dirty look, and then he realized what she had seen—Sariah's purse was on the coffee table.

To him it was not distinctive enough to identify his visitor, but Camille was a woman—or maybe she just guessed.

"You dumb shit," she said. "The lying bitch is leading you on."

"Don't call her that," he protested. "I mean it, Camille. Just don't."

"Is she still here?" She glanced around and spotted the closed bedroom door. "Oh, my God."

"Your timing sucks," he said, "but I'm glad you showed me this." It could have waited for morning, but he wanted to distract her.

"It was bad enough when you got all cozy instead of sweating the truth out of her, but *this*—"

"You don't know what this is," he said, "and it's none of your business anyway."

"Yes, it *is* my business."

"No, it isn't. You're my partner, not my mother. You don't get to decide who I spend my time off with."

"You know better—it's unprofessional for starters, and Jesus, Aaron, I never expected this from you. I am so sick of brothers who try to score points by getting a white chick—like it's some big accomplishment to fuck a pasty little honky bitch."

"Camille! That's ridiculous. Even if it wasn't totally offensive, which it is, it isn't remotely true—I'm not trying to *score.* I don't want to *get* her. And I don't care what color she is." He knew she was wrong, and yet he was guiltily aware that the contrast between his darker skin and Sariah's paleness had taken his breath away.

"Yes, you do," Camille countered. "You flirt with those Beckys every chance you get, but I didn't think you would go this far. The world is full of righteous black girls—it shouldn't be so hard to stick to your own kind."

Jesse realized Sariah was now standing in the open doorway to the bedroom. She must have heard at least part of Camille's tirade. She was prettier than ever, her cheeks flushed with anger or shame or both. Those shapely breasts were hidden under her sweater, but now he had seen them, touched them, and his gaze wanted to linger there.

"Are you jealous?" Sariah asked Camille. She sounded calmer than she appeared. "You wanted him for yourself?"

Camille made a rude noise. "As if. Trust me, Aaron is *not* my type, but that doesn't mean I don't care about his fine black ass, and a skanky white head case is not what he needs."

"Camille!" he protested. "Could you try really hard not to be such an asshole?"

Sariah was not taken aback at all. "What are you afraid of?" she asked. "Why do you object so strongly to race mixing?"

"Honey, if I have to explain it to you…"

"But can't you see it's already happened?"

Camille glared at Jesse, but that wasn't what Sariah meant.

"Look at him," she said urgently. "Are you going to tell me he doesn't have any white ancestors? It's happened, it's been happening for centuries, and *this* is the result." She pointed at Jesse. "Ugly, isn't it? Monstrous? An abomination?"

For once in her life, Camille didn't have a quick response. Sariah had said her piece too. She grabbed her purse. "Wait a minute," Jesse said. "Why are *you* leaving? Detective Farris is the one who's out of line here. Don't leave."

Sariah looked at him, but had nothing more to say. She went to the door. "Prissy little bitch," Camille said contemptuously.

"Hypocrite," Sariah returned, and the door closed behind her.

"How am I a hypocrite?" Camille demanded and before he could answer, "How could you even want to fuck *that*? World full of curvy black women, and you lust after a pale, skinny stick?"

"Yeah, well, I'll tell you what." He was too angry to make sense, but he couldn't stop himself. "Every black woman I've talked to in the last month has been a ball-buster—like you." He couldn't think of a single example, except maybe the personnel director at Maxine's, but he went right on. "You've all gotten too damn strong and independent. How is a man supposed to be a man?"

She snorted. "Well, la-di-da. Does Miss Becky fetch your slippers for you, Massa?"

"Stop it, Camille." He took a deep breath and tried to calm down. "No, Sariah is pretty damn independent too. She won't even let me into her apartment, but at least she expects me to open doors and order for her in restaurants."

"You took her *out*?"

"It is none of your business. Okay, I didn't mean any of that—I like strong women; you know I do. All the women I've been with—black women, strong black women with careers and opinions of their own—I never wanted anything else."

"Yeah, and where are they now? You dumped them."

"Erika dumped *me*," he said, "and we are not going to continue this discussion. It is *not* your business." He made an effort to compose himself and added, "We still have a murder to solve, even though you've probably alienated our only witness."

Camille had calmed down too, but couldn't resist a quick comeback: "At least I didn't try to fuck her."

"I didn't fuck her! Okay? Are you happy? Leave it alone."

"What was she doing in your bedroom?"

"Hiding from you. You scare her. You scare a lot of people. Sometimes you scare me. Now can we get back to business?" He brandished the folder under her nose.

Camille took a deep breath. "This is all the paper they could dig up, but a deputy is going to try to find more. He talked to a teacher at the school, who remembered her and thought she'd run off with a boy from Utah. She might have family who'll want to claim the body."

"I just hope they know where she went and who she might have been with."

"What does your girlfriend do for a living?" Camille asked abruptly.

"She's not my girlfriend. She works in a pet shop."

"Seriously?"

"Seriously. That's where I got the bird." He gestured toward the cage.

Camille shook her head. "She sold you a birdie along with the bill of goods? She must make good money there; that was a Louis Vuitton bag."

"She rides the bus and lives above a garage. I'm sure it was a knockoff."

"Maybe, but her sweater was cashmere."

"Women! You notice fashion details in the middle of a catfight." He wanted to dismiss it as part of her irrational tantrum, but a small doubt crept in—did Sariah have a source of income he wasn't aware of? The dress he had first seen her in was very plain, but her jeans and sweaters were more fashionable, maybe expensive, and there was the new purse and the pretty skirt and blouse she had worn to Quique's. He reminded himself she didn't have the expense of a car and her rent couldn't be very high. If she had a little spare cash, clothes were high on the list of what a woman would spend it on, and she would have had an employee discount at Maxine's. If only she wasn't so damned secretive about everything.

"Are you finished in court?" Camille asked.

"No, but maybe by tomorrow afternoon."

"Good. I'll add the possible alias to the bulletin, and then—"

"Can we strategize tomorrow? I'm not in the mood."

"Yeah, I know what you're in the mood for," Camille said. She nodded toward the folder. "That's your copy."

"Okay. Thanks for bringing it by."

She turned to go, but delivered a parting shot from the door. "Aaron—?"

"What?"

"At least use protection."

He called Sariah half an hour after Camille left. He assumed the number she had given him was a landline, the phone in the apartment above the garage, and he got the answering machine. Her voice on the recorded message was cool and businesslike—"You've reached Sariah Brennan's number. Please leave a message."

"Sariah, it's Jesse." He paused, hoping she would pick up. "I'm sorry about what happened. Can we try again? Dinner out or my apartment or whatever you want. I do want to talk to you. Call me when you get this." He repeated his number in case she had misplaced the card.

She didn't call back.

He spent a good part of the next day in court, testifying in the Thurston case, which had dragged on for almost two years now. The trial went slowly too, and he spent most of the time waiting. He had to leave his cell phone off in the courtroom, and when he was finally able to check his messages he heard Sariah's calm voice: "Java Prince. Five-thirty."

Chapter Nine

Jesse was seated at a table near the window, sipping hot, strong French roast, well before five-thirty. He speculated about Sariah's reasons for choosing a location so close to home—did it mean she was ready to let him see the apartment above the garage, or did she want to be able to make a quick exit? When she came in she was carrying a paperback book in her hand and tucked it into her purse as soon as she spotted him. She had been home to change out of her smock, so she hadn't just gotten off the bus. Maybe she'd expected him to keep her waiting. He stood up and pulled out her chair. "What'll you have?" he asked.

"I'll do it," she said and headed for the counter. Jesse studied her as she stood in line. She was wearing a simple blouse and skirt and a blue cardigan. She hadn't dressed up for him, and if they were expensive, he couldn't tell.

She returned with a cup of coffee and sat across from him. "French roast," she said. "When in Rome." She glanced around. "I know this isn't very private…"

"What are you reading?" he asked, gesturing toward her handbag. He knew nothing about her. Maybe her taste in literature would provide a clue.

"Oh, it's nothing."

This was carrying the desire for privacy a little too far. After all, she read it on public transit. She was embarrassed, and he took a shot in the dark—"What is it, *Fifty Shades of Grey*?"

"No—it's—" She pulled it out and showed him: *Harry Potter and the Chamber of Secrets.* "I know it's a children's book." She put it back in the bag, which didn't look expensive to him. What was so special about Louis Vuitton?

"Not at all," he said. "They're for all ages. I read them in my twenties."

"How old are you now?" she asked.

"Thirty-five."

"I would have guessed younger."

"Well, you know what they say." No, apparently she didn't. "Black don't crack?"

"No, I've never heard that before."

"I might be losing my hair, though."

She laughed. "It looks fine to me."

This sounded like the conversation they should have had the first time, when they were still wary of each other's motives. Now he thought—hoped—they both wanted the same thing but were unsure how to go about it. "Sariah—I'm sorry about yesterday."

"Was it meant to be good cop, bad cop?" she asked.

He was surprised and a little amused. "I didn't think of that."

"She's very good at it—bad cop."

"I'm sorry. Maybe it was. I don't think she dislikes you as much as she pretended. She admired your sweater."

"Did she?" Sariah said dryly.

"The thing is I need to work with her, and she is a good detective, but—"

"Why is it you call her Camille and she calls you Aaron?"

"She thinks Jesse is…"

"What, because it sounds the same as the girl's name?"

"Something like that."

"Try being called Sariah."

"Did you ever think of changing it?"

"Yes, but it's part of my identity."

He nodded, and they sat in silence while she tried her coffee. She was too polite to say anything. "A little strong for you?" he suggested.

"Maybe it's an acquired taste."

"I wish you hadn't left last night. I worried when I didn't hear from you. Camille was out of line, and I would have made *her* leave."

"It wasn't just bad cop," Sariah said. "I wasn't ready." She glanced around to see if they could be overheard. "I know you're used to women who can be casual about this."

Still thinking she was upset about Camille's tirade, he said, "You mean black women?"

"No," she said sharply. "I mean sophisticated, urban women. I'm not the racist here." She looked around again. "Now you can't forget I'm white, can you?"

"I can't forget anything about you," he said, "but that isn't the most important—is it?"

Sariah sipped her coffee again and set the cup down hard. "Can we go?"

He nodded and got up. He would have pulled her chair out, but she didn't wait. She was a step ahead of him until they reached the street, and she had to pause while he pointed out the car. She didn't wait for him to open the passenger door.

"Where to?" he asked. She sat with her head down and didn't answer. "We could go to my apartment, and I'll make you a cup of tea—I have some Lemon Zinger."

"I don't want to go until we've talked about some things. Can we sit here for a few minutes?"

"Sure. Sariah, if you're not ready, I won't pressure you," he promised.

"I don't want you to be disappointed," she said. She met his eyes, earnest and troubled, and he couldn't resist kissing her. She leaned into him, her lips soft and willing, and then said, "I don't have a lot of experience."

"That's not a crime." He kissed her again and rested his hand on her thigh. "I assume you don't mean…"

"I have to tell you something, before this goes any further." She was very serious and obviously uncomfortable. It occurred to him she might be about to tell the truth about Rosa Logan's murder, and part of him wanted to grab his notebook, while another part wanted to tell her *not now*. He kissed her, and she was distracted and warm, and then she pulled away and said what she had come to say: "I'm married."

Jesse took his hand off her thigh and straightened away from her. For a few seconds he was too stunned to speak. "Well, I didn't see that coming," he said. "I think you were supposed to tell me this a little sooner—like before you started taking your clothes off in my apartment. Is that what you've been hiding above the garage—a husband?"

"Of course not." She looked at him, trying to gauge his reaction. "We're separated."

"But you're still married, so it would be cheating. I guess that doesn't bother you?" *Lying, cheating…*

"Of course it bothers me, but it never came up before I met you, and I don't belong to him anymore."

"Okay, so he was controlling, and it's only been a few months…Was he abusive?"

"No, not at all. He's a good man. He let me go, but he'll never divorce me. *Never*."

"What if one of you wants to get married again?"

She had an expression he recognized from countless interrogations—she was trying to decide whether to trust him. "I won't," she said, "…and he already has."

"Wait a minute—what? He got married again, without divorcing you? Seriously? That's bigamy."

"I shouldn't have told you."

"I'm not going to go arrest him—unless you want me to."

"It's out of your jurisdiction," she said, "and it *isn't* bigamy. It's worse—or you'll think so."

"What do you mean?"

"Plural marriage. What you'd call polygamy. In Mackay it's called the Principle."

He stared at her. "No, come on, you can't be serious. You said you weren't a Mormon."

"I'm not. Mormons belong to the mainstream LDS church. They gave up plural marriage over a century ago. But a lot of independent communities still practice it."

"Jesus!… Sorry… That's insane. It's illegal, not to mention—"

"I knew you'd say that. It's an open secret in a lot of places. The government won't interfere unless abuse is reported, because it would be religious discrimination. In Mackay the police are part of the community."

"So you lived in this…community… You mean like Short Creek?"

She shook her head. "Short Creek isn't even like Short Creek. It's Colorado City now, and that was the FLDS. They're corrupt; they were led astray by a false prophet. I don't know if they'll ever find their way back."

"Wait—you bought into this? Underage marriages, women as property…?" He couldn't get his head around it.

"No—that was the FLDS. The community in Mackay is *not* like that. It's an independent group, and there are a lot of others, some a lot less conservative than Mackay. After Warren Jeffs took charge, we heard terrible things about the FLDS, scary things, probably more than you did. I told you it was corrupt."

"Racist too, I hear."

"Warren Jeffs certainly is." She straightened up and brushed away tears. "I never understood it myself. We're the same species."

"Unless you *are* from Mars. You might as well be." He shook his head. "Polygamy. That's pretty bizarre."

"Not to me. I grew up with it."

"So your father…?"

"He had two wives. A lot of men I knew had more. It seemed natural to me—until it didn't."

"And even the cops have more than one wife?"

"If they can afford it. Very few women work, and there are a lot of children to support. I suppose you think you'd like it—most men do—but it's a very hard way to live. It's supposed to be hard—a sacrifice to God."

"I guess it would be, if they made you marry some old guy."

She shook her head. "Some marriages are arranged, but nobody is forced. But you wouldn't believe what goes on—jealousy, competition, jockeying for position among the wives. It's worse than office politics, and the husband has to keep the peace and try to please everybody. Men always think it's about getting a lot of sex, but it isn't. They don't. Sex is for procreation. It's not about expressing love or giving anybody pleasure. And never when she's pregnant or nursing—which is most of the time if she's a good wife."

"And your husband…?"

"He's somebody I always loved and respected as a friend of the family. It wasn't romantic, but I never thought it would be. I wasn't pressured, but it was what was expected."

"Expectations aren't pressure?"

"Maybe. I was willing, but I wasn't very good at it. I was his third wife. The first wife had all the power, and the second was the one he loved."

"And now he has four?"

"Five. He married the fourth before I left. He'll never divorce me, because his status in heaven depends on the number of wives he has."

"Like cattle," Jesse said dismissively.

"Wives are not property," she insisted. "It's a measure of his faith."

"You believe that?" he asked. "And I suppose you're going to hell?"

"I don't believe in hell. I don't believe in much of anything anymore."

"And he was a lot older than you?"

"He just turned forty. We had sex once a week like clockwork until I got pregnant. I lost the first baby. It was supposed to be my fault...a punishment for my many sins. I wasn't receptive enough to the will of God. From the time I got pregnant with the second one until I weaned her almost two years later, he never touched me, not even a friendly pat. I think he was fond of me, but I knew he didn't desire me. He wasn't supposed to."

"So you have a daughter? What's her name?'

When she didn't answer, Jesse touched her hand gently, and she said, "I don't want to talk about her...Anna."

"Where is she?"

Sariah looked away from him, out the window. "Mackay. Now you'll say I'm an unnatural mother—"

"I wouldn't presume."

"—but she's better off where she is. She'll do well—she has the right personality for it—and she's not alone. Her father loves her, and she has other mothers. I'm just the one who gave birth to her."

"Does she know how to find you if she wants to leave?"

"She's three years old, Jesse. I think she'll be fine in Mackay—happy—but if she did want to find me, there's an organization that helps us and only a few places where most of us relocate, so it wouldn't be impossible."

He had to ask: "And Carroll City is one of those

places? So other women like you live here—women who've left…plural marriages?" He had no trouble making the leap: "Is that how you met Rosa Logan?"

The question was met with a painful silence, and then she said, "I told you I didn't know Rosa Logan." She picked her purse up from the floor. He was starting to get it—yes, escape was what she'd had in mind, in case he reacted badly.

"I'm sorry," he said, "but you both arrived from somewhere else with no record of what went before. No marriage license either, right? Legally you *aren't* married."

"No government record," she agreed. "But we had a church ceremony and a wedding certificate. It's binding in Mackay. It feels binding. He believes I'll be married to him in heaven."

Jesse didn't argue. He looked out at the street, the cars passing by, the traffic light on the corner, the Java Prince, and the bookstore next door. Everything was the same as it had been twenty minutes ago, before this bizarre revelation. "It's an amazing story," he said. "You should write a book… Is it true?"

Sariah reached for the door handle and then stopped, head down. He could see she was struggling for composure. "Yes, it's true," she said. "If you don't believe me, then don't. I had to tell you." He looked again at the street. If it was true, it had been true twenty minutes ago, and what was different now? Not the bright, cold weather or the rush of engine sounds when the light turned green. Not the woman sitting next to him or the palpable attraction between them. It *was* true—the clues had been right under his nose from the beginning: her name from the Book of Mormon, the

91

simple clothes, no alcohol or coffee. "Thanks for listening," she said. "I can walk home from here."

She opened the car door. "Sariah!" He stretched across and closed it again. "It doesn't change anything."

She studied him for a long time. "Doesn't it?"

"Why should it? Okay, so you have to adjust to a whole new way of life, and you miss your daughter, and you're dealing with the police in a strange city—no wonder you want your privacy."

Sariah was silent, but he could feel her steadying, calming herself. "I imagined things," she said. "I don't even know if they're possible. I wanted things I couldn't have in Mackay, things I wasn't supposed to want. It was wrong to want them. I don't mean just possessions, but those too. Books like *Harry Potter* weren't banned, but they weren't available. I wanted a different kind of love, physical love. After I left, I thought I could have those things, but it hasn't been easy. When I met you, I started to imagine things again. The first day, when we shook hands, I felt something—did you?"

"Not then. Later, yes."

"The women you've been with… Do you…let them catch up? Do you know what I mean?"

"Uh…yes, if I can. It's different with each one, but it's something you can work on together."

She shook her head. "That's like a foreign language to me. I know this has no future, but all I want is to feel something real."

She was right—nothing had been said about love—but he had to ask. "Why doesn't it have a future?"

"Oh, please. 'Cops don't make good domestic partners'? And I certainly don't. I have…what do they call it? Baggage. We're too different. And your family and friends would react the way bad cop did."

"It might help if you didn't call her that. She overreacted, but most people don't care anymore."

"They do when it's personal."

He was almost sure his mother would throw a conniption fit, but she would get over it. His grandmother would be cool—and none of them would know anything about it anyway, because it couldn't last. "Well, my dad…He grew up in a different time; white women were off limits. To me they were …uninteresting. Until you."

"I'm interesting?" she asked dryly, and she was so intensely real to him he couldn't resist her and leaned in for a kiss. She responded fully, warmly, and then pushed him away—not in protest, but as if something still needed to be said. "Technically it would be adultery," she said, "but emotionally, for me, it would be more like losing my virginity."

"And physically?" he asked and put his hand gently on the back of her neck to pull her close again. She kissed him back hard. "My place?" he asked.

****

Sariah barely greeted C.C. before she pressed her body against Jesse's so fiercely he could feel her bones grind against his. "Take it easy," he said. "We're not in a rush, are we?" He put his arms around her, and she relaxed a little. "Do you want to eat first?" he asked.

"No."

"You are one needy little white girl," he said.

"Why does everything have to be black or white? The 'black' actress everybody likes—Holly…?"

"You mean Halle Berry?"

"She's almost as white as I am."

"Nobody's as white as you are."

"Close your eyes, then. Or are you making fun of me again?"

He laughed, and she relaxed still more and went soft and light in his arms. "Shall we go in the bedroom, at least?" he asked. She nodded, but made no move toward it. He took her hand, led her inside, and closed the door. She took off her sweater with matter-of-fact efficiency and laid it neatly over the back of the chair. She reached for the top button of her blouse, and he said, "Let me."

They sat together on the bed, and he undid the five small buttons and kissed her parted lips. He liked the taste of her more and more. Her hair brushed against his face, and it had almost no weight or texture, like something that would blow away in the first breeze. He let one hand drift to the small of her back, and the other slipped inside her blouse and found the soft swelling under the silky fabric of the camisole.

"Jesse," she said, breathless, almost pleading. Her urgency challenged him, but he took his time removing each item of her clothing—sensible shoes, sheer stockings, long-sleeved blouse, knee-length skirt, lacy camisole, plain cotton panties. She was pale all over, down to the triangle of silky blonde hair, and her skin was soft and smooth under his hands. She was beautiful in a subtle, unexpected way, like sunlight scattered through leaves. When she was completely nude, she undressed him, staring frankly at his body as if she had never seen a man before, touching him with curious fingers. By her account, she had had sex many times, but never made love, and she deserved every consideration. He took her upturned face in both hands and gave her a slow, sensuous kiss.

"Jesse?" she said.

"Uh-huh?"

"I want to trust you."

Chapter Ten

The phone was ringing. Jesse groped for it on the bedside table and answered automatically, "Aaron," assuming someone was dead somewhere in the urban night. It was Sunday, not as prolific in violent death as Friday or Saturday, but murder didn't always obey the calendar.

"Jesse?" The voice bore strong associations—three days ago he had made love to her for the first time, and they had shared pizza and laughter and confidences on a night that still resonated deeply.

"Sariah? What's wrong?" Both the hour and the stress in her voice told him something was.

"He's there!" she said. "Now—right now!"

"Who? What are you talking about?" He was used to these sudden awakenings, but they could still be disorienting.

"Casey—K.C. At the warehouse, the same one. He's there now. You need to stop him."

"No, Sariah, you're dreaming—it was just a dream."

"No, please, you have to believe me. If I call the police, they won't go."

He sat up and turned on the bedside lamp. "Calm down. You had a vision? Maybe it was about before—it doesn't mean it's happening now."

"It's now! Jesse, please go now, before it's too

late."

"It's the middle of the night, and you're half asleep. The old cliché about returning to the scene of the crime? It doesn't happen very often in real life."

"He went back for a reason—I don't know what it is."

Camille's voice was in his head now: *You dumb shit.* "Okay, okay, I'll go take a look, all right? Go back to bed. I'll call you in the morning." He looked at the clock. It *was* morning. If he turned over and went back to sleep, Sariah would never know the difference.

"Promise?" she asked.

"Yes, I promise. Get some sleep." *One of us should.* He was still tempted to blow it off, but now he had promised. Maybe he owed her one middle-of-the-night wild goose chase. *One.* Camille was right: He was such a pussy.

The streets were quiet and not very dark. The glow of streetlights and neon reflected off the low cloud cover was as bright as moonlight. The industrial area near the shopping mall was darker. Warehouses lined the street, but he remembered which one had been the crime scene. He hadn't checked the number on his caller ID, and it occurred to him that if Sariah was neither psychic nor delusional, she might be around somewhere. *Secrets and lies.* If she had called from here, was it likely she had seen Kazimir Capek?

He parked in the alley, where it was darker and more private than the street in front of the warehouse entrance. He saw no lights, no vehicles, no open doors, no movement. Wherever K.C. was, he wasn't here, and neither was anybody else. Jesse sighed. Sariah would not be satisfied unless he got out of the car, checked the locks, looked in the windows, and generally wasted his time.

The first time he had been here was in daylight, and yellow crime scene tape had marked the perimeter. The warehouse was half full of large, flat crates, which proved to contain artwork of dubious provenance. The rest of the large space held two forklifts, a bare office with four filing cabinets, and Rosa Logan's ruined body. Sawdust on the floor had absorbed some of the blood, but there was a lot to go around. The killer had made an effort to obscure the footprints in the sawdust, but had left a partial print in the blood—new shoes of a popular brand.

Jesse got out of the car. The thunk of the door closing was loud in the silence, and although he tried to keep his footsteps quiet, the sound echoed from the buildings. The solid back door of the warehouse was fortified with a heavy lock, replacement for the one Rosa Logan's killer had broken, and the two small windows were both boarded up. He checked the boards to be sure, but they didn't give. He walked around the corner of the building, where a narrow walkway led between it and the next one. It was a little too dark to negotiate safely, so he switched on his flashlight, but kept it low, his hand half over the lens. He found nothing but blank, unmarked walls on both sides.

He emerged onto the street and turned off the flashlight. The block was partially lit by streetlights at the corners, and the illuminated signs and parking lot lights of the Plaza Center shopping mall glowed from the near distance. The front of the warehouse had a roll-up door covered by a black metal grate. A large hasp at ground level was securely padlocked.

As he straightened up after checking it, a car in front of the next building moved away from the curb with its lights off. Jesse switched on the flashlight, and the beam glinted briefly on the rear bumper. The car was a late-model compact, a Honda Civic or something similar, possibly blue. The license plate was white. He caught the first part: 7FZ—probably a recent California plate. He wouldn't be able to get back to the Interceptor in time to pursue a driver who didn't want to be followed, and he had no compelling reason to do so. He would have to tell Sariah he had missed whoever it was.

He continued his patrol of the warehouse, treading the paved space between it and the next building. The walkway was wider than the one on the other side, and enough light spilled in from the street that he kept the flashlight off even though his supposed quarry had flown. He ran his gaze over the walls on both sides and found only the lettering that identified the business next door as a garden supply wholesaler and another boarded-up window. To be thorough, he checked those boards as well.

He almost stumbled over an obstacle in his path. His first impression was of a sack of something, maybe mulch or potting soil, that gave a little as his toe caught it. He looked down and knew at once what it was—the body of a woman. For a single, awful second he thought it was Sariah. Then the flashlight was on—he didn't remember turning it on—and he could see she was African-American, about twenty, modestly dressed, with a scarf covering her hair. Her throat had been slashed, and blood had soaked her dress and spilled onto the pavement.

He leaned closer and caught his breath. She was

alive. He could hear a breathy rattle, and blood was still pulsing out. Almost without thinking, Jesse knelt with one knee pressed into her throat, reached for his cell phone with his free hand, and called 911.

****

He called Sariah from the crime scene. She answered so quickly he knew she had not taken his advice and gone back to bed. "How did you know?" he asked.

"Jesse!" Her voice was filled with relief—had she been concerned for his safety? "Did you get him?"

"No." He was numb and exhausted, unsure where to begin. He had scrubbed at his hands with hand sanitizer as obsessively as an OCD surgeon, but the coppery smell of blood was everywhere, especially on his clothes. "I'm sorry. I was too late, but I have a lead on the car. We'll follow up on it tomorrow. I just wanted you to know it's being taken care of and you can go back to sleep. We'll talk about it tomorrow."

"There's something you're not telling me."

"I'm sure there are a lot of things I'm not telling you. Like you're not telling me how you knew. If you're really psychic, you know what happened. I'd like to go to bed now, and I suggest you do the same."

She didn't answer, and after a few seconds of silence on the line she hung up.

Camille had walked up while he was on the phone and was signing the logbook. He braced himself for an assault on his stretched nerves. "Dead hooker?" she asked.

He shook his head. "Not a hooker, and last I heard she wasn't dead."

"Then why are we here?"

"Because she had her throat slashed like Rosa Logan, probably by the same perp—and did you notice where we are? His car was parked on the street." He pointed. "I got a partial plate—7FZ."

"Which narrows it down to—what? Twenty-six hundred suspects?"

"Something like that. We can limit it by geography and the car description—I think it was a blue Honda Civic."

She finally absorbed what he was saying. "*You* think—you're the witness? What were you doing here—in the middle of the night—without me? If you got a tip…"

"It's a long story."

"I bet. Why would he kill another gal in the same place?"

"Maybe she can tell us—if she lives. You ever see a victim survive having her throat cut?"

"Not personally, but I've heard of it happening. A cop I worked with had a partner who recovered from a pretty deep cut. Scar from here to here," she added, gesturing graphically. "Don't guess this vic will be able to talk to us any time soon. You have her ID?"

"No, none on her—no purse. She doesn't look old enough to have pissed anybody off, and I don't think she'd been sexually assaulted, but we should check missing persons in case he held her for a while."

Camille took a step back and looked him over. "That her blood on you?" She didn't wait for an answer. "You look like a friggin' butcher. What did you do?"

"Called 911 and tried to keep her from bleeding out before the paramedics arrived." Remembering it made him feel weak in the knees, but he couldn't let her see that. "I guess he didn't sever the jugular."

"And you were here…why?"

"I just…I got a tip, okay? I didn't call you because I didn't think it was credible. I almost didn't check it out." He could imagine the regret, not to mention the condemnation from Sariah, if he had gone back to sleep. Right now he felt as if he would never sleep again.

"You do remember we're partners, don't you?" Camille asked and then, in disgust, "Go home and change your clothes. I've got this."

He went home and showered and lay down for a couple of hours, but didn't sleep much. He couldn't yet grapple with the facts of the case or how deeply Sariah must be involved, but only try to block the flashes of memory—the woman's ravaged throat, her slack face in the circle of light, the staggering moment when he thought it might be Sariah, the scent of blood, the glimpse of the fleeing car, Camille's acerbic words: *You do remember we're partners, don't you?*

Chapter Eleven

After two cups of coffee, Jesse dressed in a conservative, dark blue suit with a blue-and-silver tie, but when he looked for the silver cufflinks that went best with the tie, he couldn't find them. When had he worn them last—in court the other day? He laughed at himself—he should be too young to start misplacing things. The stress must be getting to him.

When he arrived at headquarters, the list from the DMV database of likely 7FZ license plates was on his desk. It was short enough for one to immediately stand out: a blue 2010 Kia Forte registered to Elisabeth Wilson. He updated the BOLO he had put out on the partial plate, accessed her license information, and picked up the phone to call Camille at the hospital. Elisabeth Faith Wilson was twenty-one, African-American, five foot three and 120 pounds. He couldn't tell whether it was the same girl, but what were the odds? Camille's phone was off, which he hoped meant she had been allowed to see their victim, who was unconscious and in critical condition in the ICU.

He had barely hung up when Sariah got off the elevator. She wore a blue-and-green print dress and the same blue cardigan she had taken off in his apartment Thursday night. The dress was uncharacteristic but very nice, and her hair was in a French braid. She was dressed up for something—he didn't imagine it was him. Her makeup—lipstick and mascara—had been applied with subtle care, and she was wearing a delicate floral scent. She looked very chic and very dignified, but it was impossible not to remember her in a completely different way.

When her eyes met his, she flushed—almost as if she could read his mind. She entered, but didn't speak, waiting for him to begin. "Good morning," he said. "You look nice. What are you dressed up for?"

"A job interview."

"You're leaving World of Wings?'

"Cleaning cages gets old."

"Sariah...I'm sorry if I was abrupt last night—or this morning I guess it was."

"You were angry," she said. "I woke you up in the middle of the night."

He hit Print and got up to retrieve the page. He held it out to her, with his other hand covering the identifying information. "Do you know who this is?"

She studied it, taking it seriously, but showed no sign of recognition. "I hope it's not your girlfriend." She meant it as a joke, but her voice caught.

Jesse took his hand away. She looked up at him, her face alight. "You found her."

"*You* found her. You saved her life last night." He pointed to the chair in front of his desk. "Have a seat." She sat down and waited while he came around behind the desk. He remained standing and used his sternest voice: "Ms. Brennan, I don't want to take you in there"—indicating the interrogation room—"and sweat it out of you. I need you to tell me what you know."

"I did."

"No, you did not." He moved abruptly toward her

104

and slammed his fist down on the desk. Papers fluttered, and Sariah jumped. Michelle glanced their way, but she was on the phone and immediately distracted. "I can play bad cop too," he said. Sariah looked up at him, a visible pulse beating in her throat, her eyes wide.

She said the last thing he expected: "I didn't thank you for the flowers."

"Sariah!" He sat down. "You have to take this seriously. A young woman was almost killed last night. For all I know, you might be next. I'm in a very tricky position here—I've let this go on too long, and if it comes out that I—that we—"

She frowned. "You could get in trouble?"

He sighed. "I could get fired. Do you want to go in there?" He pointed to the interrogation room again, with as much threat in his manner as he could manage.

"I told you the truth," she said. "I'm sorry you don't believe me."

"I *can't*. It isn't credible. What the hell am I going to do about this?"

"Catch him."

"I'm trying. He stole Ms. Wilson's car." He sat back and studied her. He had no idea what to do. He knew nothing about her. Thursday night, in a warm, confiding afterglow, she had talked freely about her "plig" childhood—and nothing else. He gestured again toward the interrogation room and asked, "Want to fool around? We can close the blinds."

Sariah smiled. He loved her smile. "Another time," she said. "I only have a few minutes before my interview."

"Where is it?"

"The Studio West art gallery—do you know it?"

"I've seen the building. Impressive. I hope you get it. But who will I go to for bird advice?"

"I'll moonlight," she promised. Her gaze fell on the printout again, and she tapped the photo. "He likes black girls too," she said. "K.C."

"You think he wanted to kill her because he liked her?"

"I think he did at one time. It was a crime of passion."

"You can't know that, even if you were there," he said. "You're romanticizing. Unless he told you—like he told you where he was going to be last night?"

Sariah shrugged. "I know you don't believe that," she said. She studied the picture of Elisabeth Wilson. "She's pretty, isn't she?"

"Not bad," he agreed. He couldn't help seeing her as he had last night—her face a ghastly, greenish shade, blood gushing from her slender throat.

"Jesse?" Sariah was very serious.

"What?"

"If we're going to continue with this, I want you to know—if I'm not enough for you, it's all right. We don't have to be exclusive. I'm used to sharing."

"Okay," he said when he could speak calmly, "but just so *you* know—I'm not. One at a time is about all I can handle."

"What happened with your old girlfriend?" she asked.

"What happened at Maxine's?" he countered. She didn't respond in any way. "You make me crazy, Sariah."

"In a good way?"

"In every way."

Behind her he saw Camille get off the elevator and stop to chat with Michelle. "Uh-oh," he said. "The queen of bad timing."

Sariah turned. "She's better at bad cop than you are, too," she said. Her earlier near-panic in Camille's presence was gone. "Why aren't you her type?" she asked.

"She likes them big and dumb. I mean bigger and dumber than me. The newest one is a football player."

"She should get married and settle down. It might improve her personality."

"Did it improve yours?" he asked.

She didn't answer. When Camille came in, she got up in no apparent hurry. "Good day, Detective Farris," she said coolly.

"Nice shoes," was all Camille had to say.

"Thank you," Sariah said and, in parting, to Jesse, "Thank you for the flowers."

Camille stood with one hand on her hip and her eyebrows raised and watched her walk toward the elevator. Jesse looked too—he liked watching her. Her shoes were low heels and matched her handbag, but he didn't see anything special about them. "La-di-da," Camille said. She turned on him, frowning. "You sent her flowers?"

"Good morning, Camille."

"Yeah, good morning. Jesus, you did her, didn't you? And flowers the morning after? How quaint. So how was she? Did you make her squeak? I bet she's a squeaker."

"*Camille*," he said, with all the dignity he could muster. Rising to the bait would only make her worse.

"There is a reason bedrooms have doors." She snorted. Jesse dodged whatever else she might want to say by handing her the printout of Elisabeth Wilson's driver's license. "That her?"

"Yeah, probably. She's not at her best right now. She doesn't have any defensive wounds—maybe he hit her on the head first. They did a CT scan but don't think she has a serious brain injury. Obviously saving her life took precedence over forensics, but they did the best they could for us. It was probably the same kind of knife used on Logan, a right-handed cut. She had tape marks on her wrists. She wasn't vaginally raped, but they found semen in her mouth. Anything on the car?"

"It's hers—so did he take her to the warehouse in it or steal it after he killed—tried to kill her? I didn't see any other cars nearby, but I should check again today. CSU is still processing the crime scene."

"Okay, but before you head out, I need to get something off my chest."

"Shoot," he said and leaned back in his chair.

"There's an opening in Northwestern Division. I'm thinking seriously about asking to be reassigned."

"*What?*"

"Yeah. If we can't trust each other…"

"I do trust you. I always have."

"Not lately. You think I don't know you've been holding out on me? And I can't trust you, because you've got your head muddled by Miss Tinker Bell. You are blinded by the light, my friend. I know how it is with new love—"

Jesse shook his head. "I don't believe in this psychic crap, but I can't get anything out of her. It doesn't mean I'm in love with her."

"You will be."

"No, I'm just trying to figure her out."

"Yeah, I always send flowers to reluctant witnesses myself. Aaron, you had sex with her. Don't try to tell me you didn't. In case you hadn't heard, women do men they fall in love with, but men fall in love with women they have sex with."

"Nice theory, but—"

"Even if you could keep from getting emotionally entangled, it's wrong on every level."

"Not the race thing again."

"Yeah, okay, I was pissed because she's white, but now I'm worried for you. You're letting her override your good judgment, and why? Because she acts all helpless and lets you open doors? Bats her eyelashes at you?"

"Come on, Camille. She knows something she can't tell us, but she's given us a lot."

"You're into some deep shit here, brother. You haven't been straight with me, so I can't help. Let *me* question her, and we'll get to the bottom of it quick enough. *I'm* not hankering after her little white ass."

"You'll eat her alive. She's had a rough time, left a bad marriage, a bad situation, and she had a child…"

"So fucking what?" She glanced toward Michelle and lowered her voice. "So effing what? Who hasn't had a rough time? You're gonna save her and wrap her up in cotton batting?"

"She's too tough to let me."

"Tougher than you anyway. Let me take a crack at her."

"I'll…I'll handle it."

"Yeah, right."

"If Wilson can talk to us, it won't matter anyway."

"While we're waiting for her, our perp is getting in the wind."

"I'll talk to Sariah again…tonight."

"Oh, *Su-ry-ah*! What, in bed? Yeah, you can really play hardball, huh? You could at least give me everything you have instead of trying to protect her."

"I'm not."

She shook her head. "Northwestern is sounding better and better."

"That's blackmail."

"No, that's me getting fed up. Tell me what you have, and I'll see what I can do with it. Tomorrow I take Brennan into the interrogation room and get to the bottom of this, so if you think you can crack her, get it done tonight."

"I don't think I have anything you can use," he said, but he paged through his notebook for something he could give her. The effort wasn't police work; it was a peace offering. "I talked to her landlady, her employer, her previous employer…"

"I'll talk to them again. Tell me what you got."

He ran down the facts and gave her a short version of what Sariah had told him. She took out her notebook and wrote it all down.

"Jeez—polygamy? She can spin a tale, can't she?"

"I think it's true."

"She was in a *cult*?"

"I don't think it's a cult. It's a different way of life—and not strictly legal."

"Boy, you sure know how to pick 'em. Polygamy in Idaho? Give me a break. I've heard of fringe groups in Utah—not Idaho. She played you—again. Did you call this Mackay?"

"The police are locals, and they all protect each other. The state didn't have anything."

"Okay, and she was fired from Maxine's?"

"Dismissed…they say for cause. She says it was a misunderstanding."

"What was the cause?" She correctly interpreted his shrug. "Jeez, Aaron. I guess I'll start there."

He shook his head. "I talked to the personnel director. She wanted to lawyer up right away."

"She's not a suspect, genius. Grow some balls."

"I'll—"

"You'll back off. You're useless. I've got this." Shaking her head, she left the room.

After that, going back to the warehouse was a picnic. He hadn't had much sleep and had a headache, and the fresh air helped. He talked to the Crime Scene Unit and employees of the businesses in the area and ran the plates of every car within six blocks. As with the Logan murder, the security camera showed nothing of interest, and the warehouse manager was convincingly clueless and very disturbed by the violence. Jesse had better luck with an employee, who glanced at Capek's mug shot and said, "Oh, that guy."

"You know him?"

"No, but I seen him. I don't remember the scar, but yeah. He tried to sell me some stolen goods once. I shut him down."

"When was this?"

"Dunno. Four, five months ago?"

"He give you a name?"

"No, man, I told you I shut him down."

"You call the police?"

"About some crappy chains? His word against mine anyway, and I had work to do."

"If you see him again, give me a call," Jesse said, handing him a card.

Between interviews, he took a call from Sariah. "It went very well," she said. "I think I'll probably get the job."

"That's great," he said. "How about if I take you out to dinner tonight to celebrate?"

"It might be a little premature. They'll call me, but it might be a few days."

"Let's do it anyway." He felt a little guilty—she was so happy, and he had ulterior motives. "You choose the place, and I'll pick you up—six?"

"Six-thirty. I'd like to try Quique's again, if you don't mind."

"Fine with me. Bring a sweater, and we'll sit on the patio. It might be chilly, but they have space heaters at the tables."

His next call was all business—the Thurston jury was in. He didn't have to go, but he could easily make time to. The verdict proved to be the best part of his workday—guilty on two counts of first-degree and one count of second-degree murder. Thurston had slaughtered his ex-wife's family, but the evidence was spotty, so it wasn't a foregone conclusion. He left satisfied justice had been done and he could concentrate on Sariah tonight.

Chapter Twelve

Quique's wasn't crowded, and Jesse and Sariah were shown to a good table on the patio. The evening was mild, so the space heaters weren't on, and her bulky gray sweater was comfortably warm. She was wearing a shorter skirt than usual, in a matching gray, and a silky red blouse with the top button undone. She had taken her hair out of the French braid and brushed it straight, but it still showed a hint of wave. She looked very pretty and absolutely guileless.

She noticed the large, colorful margaritas at other tables and suggested he order one and let her try a little. Not a good idea—he needed a clear head tonight—but it was part of Quique's ambience, and one wouldn't hurt. He ordered a small strawberry margarita and an iced tea for Sariah. She took a little longer with the menu this time and decided on chimichanga. Jesse ordered steak picado, and she asked, "How's your blood pressure?"

"I'm sure it's fine," he said, although he felt as if it was rising by the minute.

She took a tiny, ladylike sip of his margarita. "Well," she said dubiously.

"It's an acquired taste," he said.

They talked casually at first. Sariah told him more about the art gallery job—she thought she would enjoy it and was confident about the interview.

"You looked good anyway," he said, and she smiled her gratitude.

He told her about the Thurston verdict. She didn't want to hear the details of the murders, but was pleased his hard work had not been wasted by a soft jury.

"Sariah…" he said seriously.

"Uh-oh," she said, still smiling. "Here it comes. The third degree."

"I'd rather not, but Camille will lean on you hard tomorrow if I don't."

"*Lean* on me?"

"I'm not joking. What she will do is barge into World of Wings and make a scene guaranteed to make you glad you have another job lined up, because you won't want to go back—stop smiling; I'm serious."

"Okay," she said, trying for a sober expression. "But you are so—"

Exasperated: "What?"

Sariah blushed and lowered her voice. "Sexy."

He was nonplussed and then said, "You won't be able to distract Camille like you do me. She will—"

"All right! You ask me, then. I'm tired of being pressured to lie. I've already told the truth."

"All of it?"

"I explained about the phone—and it didn't matter, did it? You were just being paranoid."

"I'm not paranoid. I'm frustrated because I can't get through to you. Is everything you told me—including the second version about the phone—the truth?"

"Yes."

"All of it?"

"Yes! I said yes."

"Polygamy in Idaho?"

"Why would I make it up? I didn't want to tell you, but I had to. You already didn't believe me, and I knew how bizarre you would think it was. That was your word, bizarre, and it was my life; I lived it."

"What's your husband's name?"

"You don't need to know his name."

"I need to know what the truth sounds like."

"What does *that* mean?" She took a long swallow of iced tea, buying time for both of them to calm down. "I don't want to have an argument. I thought we were going to have a nice dinner."

He tried another approach. "Camille is threatening to transfer because she thinks I'm blowing this."

"Wouldn't you be better off with another partner? She's so mean."

He would have defended Camille, but he preferred to let Sariah fear her right now. "That's not the point. I can handle her, and we work well together—most of the time anyway. But I don't want her to start on you, Sariah. She *will* get what she wants, and she will want everything, including what happened between you and me, and yes, it is relevant, because getting involved with a witness is a serious breach of ethics."

"She already knows what happened. Let her try. I don't care."

It was his turn to take a drink to buy time. The margarita was icy and sweet. "You've changed a lot since you came to see me the first time."

"Not really. It takes me a while to get used to new people."

"Or you were putting on an act?"

"No, and I haven't changed. I stopped being afraid

of your partner when I realized what a hypocrite she is."

"She's a good cop."

"So you say, but she hasn't found K.C. either, has she? Could I try a bite of your steak?"

"Yes, but stop trying to distract me. You *have* changed."

"What do you want, Jesse? I didn't change; I just revealed more of myself. Of course I'm different with you now. Weren't the other women you've been with different when you got to know them? When you made love to them? I told you it would be a big deal for me. I'd never been with anyone except my husband, and it was no good with him."

"So you just had to have decent sex once, and your whole personality—"

"If you'll remember…"

"Okay, twice."

She glanced toward the nearest diners, leaned forward, and lowered her voice. "It was more than decent I think…for me, anyway."

"You're doing it again."

She raised her eyebrows in a parody of innocence.

"Trying to distract me."

Sariah sighed. "My husband's name is Levi. Levi Gilbert Smith."

"Smith?"

"Smith. Which you may know is a very common name, not least in polygamous circles. I didn't make it up. Joseph Smith, remember? You can call Mackay and talk to him—Levi, not Joseph Smith—but don't tell him where I am. He won't come after me, but I don't want him to know. You said yourself the government won't have a record of the marriage, and he won't trust you, but I can't help that, can I?"

"I don't have to talk to him. I just wanted you to stop hiding."

"What about you? Isn't it my turn? What was your last girlfriend's name?"

"I'm not the witness here… Okay, her name was Erika."

"What was the dog's name?"

"Sariah…"

"What was the dog's name? Maybe I want to hear what the truth sounds like too."

"Rusty. Male golden retriever. Not very original, but it's the truth."

"Why did you and Erika break up?"

"It's complicated."

"Life usually is."

"She broke it off. I'll give you a tip—never plan a wedding too elaborate to back out of. It gets very ugly."

"You were going to get married?"

"It sure looked like it. Doesn't matter now, does it?"

"No, but…I'm sorry." She gave him a look full of sympathy and sadness, and he wanted to kiss her and let everything else go. He pushed a bit of steak toward the edge of his plate, and she took it on her fork with an appreciative murmur. His eyes lingered on her mouth. What was it he needed to ask?

"Did you witness the murder of Rosa Logan?"

"Wham!" she said. "No."

"How did you know K.C. was at the warehouse last night?"

"I don't know. I just knew."

"You were sure enough to get me out of bed in the middle of the night, so you must have had strong reasons to think so." These questions would have been easier to ask before he held her in his arms. He looked away for a moment to steady himself and caught a stare from a neighboring table. Was he being too loud? Or just too black?

Sariah sighed. "I was right, wasn't I?"

"Well, *somebody* was at the warehouse and did the same thing to Elisabeth Wilson."

"What do you mean? You stopped him, didn't you? He didn't kill her."

"He cut her throat. She survived, but she could still die. Thanks to you, I got there in time to call 911, and the paramedics were able to keep her alive."

Her eyes widened. "You didn't tell me he hurt her."

"It wasn't in your vision?"

She didn't answer. She was obviously shocked, but also annoyed at yet another dig. Finally she asked, "Did he put her finger in his mouth?"

"Not as far as I know, but she wasn't wearing a wedding ring."

He shouldn't have said it. She made the connection. "Oh, with Rosa Logan it was her ring finger... He...?"

"We don't know for sure, but it's likely he removed her wedding ring with his teeth. Camille has been checking the pawn shops, but it hasn't shown up."

"He won't sell it," she said.

"How do you know?"

She shrugged. "I don't know."

"How convenient. You hadn't had a lot of

experience with these visions coming true. What made you confident enough to talk to the police about this one?"

"I *wasn't* confident," she said, "but I had to do it."

"When did you first know it was Capek? You didn't know Rosa, but you saw her picture in the paper?"

"No, before—when I saw her picture I knew who she was and that I could go to the police, but I already knew what he did to her."

"Tell me about the vision."

She lowered her eyes. "Blood. Everywhere. He was bending over her."

"But it wasn't like a dream? Did you see a blinding light, a flash, or did you hear sounds or feel pain, as if you were having a seizure or something?"

"I just saw what I saw."

"The story about your brother? Was it true?"

"Yes."

"But you only heard his voice? You didn't see anything?"

"I knew where he was, so maybe I did. My grandmother told me I said, 'Andy's in the well.'"

"You don't remember saying it?"

She sighed. "It would be easier to explain if I thought you would believe me, but you're so sure I'm lying and keep trying to trip me up. It's very annoying, because I trusted you—I still trust you. Bad cop is egging you on—"

"Don't call her that."

The waitress chose that moment to ask cheerfully if everything was all right and if they would like anything else. "More iced tea?"

"No, thank you," Sariah said. "Could I have one of those?" She gestured toward the margarita.

"Sure. A small strawberry?"

"One like that," she said, pointing to another table.

"A large lemon lime?"

"Yes. Please."

"What are you doing?" he asked when the waitress was gone.

"Having a new experience," she said. "*This* one is getting old."

"You don't even like the taste, and you're not used to it. You'll get drunk."

"Good. I'm not driving."

"Sariah—I know what you're doing. You're trying to distract me again."

"I wish I could. Why don't you want me to drink? *In vino veritas*—and you can have your way with me…Smile. It was a joke."

She drank every drop. He made sure she ate all of her chimichanga, and ordered dessert and coffee. Her voice got a little louder and her face a little flushed, but she didn't spill any secrets. She didn't slur her words or get silly or mean. He was ready to tell Camille it wasn't his fault; Sariah was too damn tough.

When they left the restaurant, she was a little unsteady on her feet but seemed sober enough. He didn't want to take her home and have her stumble on the stairs, or at least that was what he told himself. "You'd better spend the night at my place," he said.

She was very cheerful when they got to his apartment. He didn't assume they would make love, but maybe she did. Or maybe she thought the interrogation was over. He switched on the Keurig while she was using the bathroom. When she came back she said, "I couldn't drink any more coffee. I've had more than enough."

"I don't think so."

"I'm not drunk." She glanced around the kitchen. "Your apartment is so neat," she said. "Aren't bachelors supposed to be messy?"

"I guess I'm not here enough to make much of a mess," he said. She watched while he took out mugs and selected K-Cups. Jesse didn't ask her to choose, but gave her the strongest coffee he had.

"I should get one of those," she said.

"You don't drink coffee," he reminded her. "It's a Mormon tenet, isn't it?"

She shrugged. "It was the way we did things in Mackay. Caffeine is very unhealthy. Your body is a temple."

Jesse handed her a brimming mug. "Drink that. It'll put hair on your chest…no, I guess not."

Sariah laughed and took a sip. "Ouch," she said. He gestured for her to go ahead of him into the living room. She set her mug on the coffee table and went to chirrup to C.C. Jesse joined her and then covered the cage and led her back to the couch. She glanced around and asked, "Did Erika live here with you?"

"Sort of." He did not want to talk about Erika. "How about you? Did you all live together in one house with Smith and all the wives?"

"We had two houses. I lived with Zilpah and later Vivian."

"Zilpah?"

"Biblical names are popular. The children were back and forth all the time."

"Do you miss her? Anna?"

"I miss all the children," she admitted. "The grownups not so much. I never pleased *anybody*. I was always too much or too little of whatever they wanted me to be. If one appreciated something I did, somebody else would hate it. Levi lived with Esther in the other house. Sometimes we would go there for meals, birthday parties, Bible readings, and so on, or they would come to our house. Sometimes he would come alone for dinner or to see the children, but I was almost never alone with him except on our nights—in the bedroom with at least one sister wife in the house. We could talk privately then, but we weren't supposed to have secrets."

"It sounds very strange."

"Mostly it was tedious." She met his eyes gravely. "I don't know what a normal relationship is like. Is this one?"

"I don't know what this is. I know it shouldn't be happening, not until this case is wrapped up. How do I convince you to come clean with me?"

She sighed. "Can't we just..." She leaned forward to brush his lips with hers. "For one night, couldn't we pretend none of this matters? I'm so tired of these questions."

"I'm getting tired of the answers myself, but it does matter. Even if I could let it go, Camille won't, and what I don't find out tonight—"

"Good cop, bad cop again."

"Damn it, Sariah, we can't go on like this. Your story is not credible, and I have to know what really happened."

"K.C. killed Rosa Logan and tried to kill Elisabeth

Wilson. Go find him and stop raising your blood pressure because you don't like the way you got the information."

"You must have some connection with Casey. You know him, or somebody who does. Maybe his wife?"

She shook her head. "I told you the truth. If it's not credible to you, maybe you're the problem. If you were more open minded…" She kissed him again and then reached to set her mug on the coffee table. "I can't drink this. It's horrible. You can believe this is delicious and somehow good for you, but you can't believe God gave me a gift to help you solve your case?"

"You said you didn't believe in anything anymore."

She sighed. "I don't know what to believe." She got up. "I'm going home. I'll take the bus."

"You don't need to do that. If you want to go, I'll drive you home, but I don't think you should climb those stairs tonight."

"I'm not drunk. It was one margarita. I'm fine. I thought we could have a nice evening instead of you badgering me again." She picked up her purse and started toward the door. "If you want to do bad cop's dirty work, at least don't act as if we can have a relationship when all you want is to grill me."

Jesse went after her and grabbed her arm. "I need you to tell me the truth," he said angrily.

"I did. I need you to believe me." She gave him an intense, beseeching look. Her purse dropped to the floor, and she took his face in her hands. "Let it go," she said and kissed him hard.

Time was running out, and he had nothing. He was

risking his career by being with her, risking his partnership by failing, feeling more frustrated than he ever had in his life. He shoved her against the wall, unbuttoned her blouse, and pulled up her skirt.

"No, Jesse," she said, tugging it back down. "Please don't, not when you're angry."

"I'm not angry," he lied. "You said you wanted to feel something real." *He* was feeling something real, something he had never felt with any woman and rarely with suspects—a desire, not to hurt, but to subdue, not because it was the job, but because he wanted to.

She didn't resist, didn't protest again, let him take her into the bedroom and push her down on the bed, still only half undressed. She held onto the headboard with both hands instead of embracing him, but he sensed no reluctance in the way her body yielded to his. They were not making love; she was simply accommodating him. She wasn't angry or afraid, but when their eyes locked, he saw an intense emotion he couldn't identify.

When he was finished, he lay beside her and listened to her ragged breathing. He didn't feel anything, not even physical relief, certainly not as if he had subdued anything in her, and at first not much in the way of regret. The worst part was he was still angry.

"It's all right," she said, but it wasn't. Now he realized what he had seen in her eyes. He had encountered it many times on the job—in the faces of prostitutes. Boredom—a deep weariness with the foolishness of men. She was used to this—not the anger, but the failure to engage her fully as a partner.

"I'm sorry," he said.

"It's okay. You didn't hurt me. Is this the end?"

"Of what?"

"Everything. Us."

He reached out and put his hand on her hair and after a moment pulled her toward him and kissed the top of her head, her forehead, her eyes. "Sorry, sweet," he said.

"I like that—sweet."

He felt worse by the minute. All she had ever asked of him was to let her catch up, and he had done *this*, and she liked him using a meaningless endearment—or maybe not meaningless; he had felt something when he said it, even if it was remorse. "Sorry," he murmured again. He stroked her pale, soft belly, and she shivered with what he hoped was pleasure.

"You owe me one," she said.

He undressed her completely, taking his time. He always did his best to pay his debts.

Chapter Thirteen

Jesse woke to the sound of the shower running. His head throbbed—stress, lack of sleep, a pressing crowd of painful thoughts. He wished everything was less complicated. He glanced at the clock, but didn't move. He contemplated joining Sariah in the shower. Would she like it if he did, or consider it an invasion of privacy?

He got up and put on the black fleece robe Erika had given him for Christmas. Sariah's clothes were draped over the back of the chair, and her purse sat open on the seat. He was sure it had been in the living room last night, so she had retrieved it and taken something out. He couldn't help himself. He didn't even have to open it, and she would never know.

The contents proved unexceptional. A bifold wallet held her California ID card, library card, bus pass, one credit card, and less than twenty dollars in cash. It was leather, but didn't look very expensive. A mirrored compact, lipstick, mascara, a key ring with three keys—work, home, and…? A pack of sugar-free gum, a roll of Lifesavers, a packet of Kleenex, a ballpoint pen, an emery board, fashionable sunglasses he had never seen her wear. A zippered compartment concealed tampons and her passport—recent, with the same information as her ID and a better picture. No checkbook with a suspicious balance to suggest she had cashed Mrs.

Capek's checks, no cell phone he could check for revealing numbers. The shower turned off. He made sure he hadn't disturbed anything and left the purse as he had found it.

When she emerged she was pink from the steamy shower and wearing nothing but one of his white shirts and a towel wrapped around her hair. "Fetching outfit," he said.

Sariah smiled. "Good morning," she said. She gestured toward the bathroom. "All yours."

He went to her and kissed her, and she slid her hands inside the robe to stroke his bare chest. "Nice," she murmured and kissed him back.

"I don't think we have time for that. We both have to go to work, right?"

"Yes," she said, but her fingers lingered, a soft, light touch against his skin.

He took her hands and held each palm briefly to his lips. "Don't tempt me," he said.

When he came out of the bathroom, she had made the bed with clean sheets and laid out clothes for him, but she was still in his shirt. He didn't object to what she had chosen for him, but it struck him as a tad presumptuous. Had she done this for her husband?

"Get dressed," he said. "I'll scramble some eggs or something."

"I couldn't eat eggs. Oatmeal maybe. Do you have any aspirin?"

"You said you didn't take aspirin. Hangover?"

"I guess. I'll be sure to tell bad cop how you got me drunk and took advantage of me."

"You need to stop calling her that. Are you going to get dressed?"

She took off his shirt. No, there was nothing unripe about her body. This might be a hard habit to break.

****

He didn't see Camille all morning, but she called from the hospital in early afternoon to bring him up to date. Elisabeth Wilson was still unconscious, she told him, still critical. Waiting for her to be able to speak to them was excruciating. "Tell me you know what I'm going to say next," Camille said sternly.

"How would I—?"

"Because you did your job last night maybe?"

"Just tell me what you found out."

"Miss Personnel Director sang like a canary—did you even *try*?"

"Give me a break, Camille. It was a long night."

"Yeah, I bet. It seems certain items went missing on Brennan's watch."

"Missing?" This was starting to sound familiar. He still hadn't found the silver cufflinks. He was sure he had misplaced them, but something nagged at him. Nobody had been in his apartment except Camille, the weekly cleaning lady he had used for years...and Sariah.

"Yep. Not only that, she had another 'misunderstanding' with another store. Your girlfriend is *persona non grata* at the shopping center. They were about an inch from getting a restraining order."

"That's absurd. She's—"

"She's a *thief*."

"Wait a minute, wait a minute..." He tried to process this, tried to remember what Sariah had said. She wanted things she couldn't have, not just possessions—had she said "but those too"? Had she helped herself to things she couldn't afford? The expensive coat, the smart dress and shoes for the interview, the Louis Vuitton bag? "There couldn't be anything to this," he said. "The stores would have pressed charges."

"The Maxine's items turned up—"

"So it *was* a misunderstanding."

"—after she was accused. The other store's stuff didn't, but they weren't sure it was her."

"Well, then…"

"A few other stores remembered seeing her, but hadn't suspected anything, so I requested their surveillance tapes. They don't go back as far as the Maxine's incident, but she's on some of the recent ones and can be seen liberating enough specific items to list on an affidavit. I just got word the judge is ready to sign the search warrant for her apartment, so I'm heading there now. I'll keep you informed, but it's better if you're not involved."

"No. I'll go with you." Should he? Get a grip, he told himself. "If there's anything to find, I want to see it for myself."

"Meet me at the courthouse, then," she said. "Do not go to her place ahead of me. Seriously, do *not*!"

"No, I won't." He was starting to feel numb.

"And if you call and warn her, I swear to God, Aaron, I will report you to Internal Affairs myself."

"Okay, but reserve judgment until we see—"

"Take your own advice," she said and hung up.

He wanted to call back and ask why they should pursue this. If Sariah was guilty of shoplifting, what did it have to do with their case? The warehouse was full of artworks, and Kazimir Capek had offered stolen goods to an employee. Sariah was seeking a job at an art gallery. Was Capek a fence? Or was all of this irrelevant, a red herring? Camille was more than willing to discredit the woman who had distracted him from any other avenue of investigation, but she had not created the evidence on the surveillance tapes. Sariah was a thief.

Chapter Fourteen

Sariah wasn't home. Jesse and Camille went to the Dunwoods' door, and Peggy answered it. "Mister Detective!" She sounded pleased. "Come on in."

"We don't need to come in," Camille told her. She showed her badge and patted her jacket pocket. "We have a warrant to search your garage apartment. I assume you have a key?"

"Say *what*?" She was asking Jesse, but he had agreed to let Camille take the lead and deferred to her. "Well, okay," Peggy said and went inside.

"Mister Detective?" Camille said when she was out of earshot. "Did you flirt with her too? Isn't she a little obvious?"

"She flirted with me."

"You didn't have to respond."

"I didn't."

Peggy returned with the key. "My goodness," she said when she spotted the patrol car and the two officers who had arrived to assist in the search. "Whatever is going on? Is Sariah here? Shouldn't we have her permission?"

"That won't be necessary," Camille said smoothly, "but we do appreciate *your* cooperation. If you'll open the door for us, we'll take it from there. Please do *not* contact Ms. Brennan."

Peggy glanced nervously at Jesse. "I don't know if

I could," she said. "Does this have something to do with *special abilities*?"

Camille gave her a blank look and gestured toward the stairs. They waited while Peggy climbed up and unlocked the door. She glanced inside and came back down, apparently mystified. She started to ask Jesse a question, but Camille cut her off. "We'd appreciate it if you waited inside your residence." She motioned to the patrol officers, and the four of them headed up the stairs, armed with lists and evidence bags.

Jesse hesitated in the doorway.

Sariah had been so adamant about not letting him in. He was trying to let go of her, distance himself emotionally, but this was still an unwarranted invasion of her privacy—and unwarranted was definitely the wrong word. He went in.

He didn't know what he expected. A shrine to her daughter? Fugitive plural wives? He had imagined a studio, but it was a large one-bedroom apartment with living and dining areas and a full kitchen. It seemed quite ordinary at first glance and then admittedly a little cluttered—not *Hoarders* material, but too many objects for the space. Sunlight spilled in through the large windows, and it was clean and bright, but it contained too many *things*.

She had a TV—not large or expensive-looking— which might have belonged to the furnished apartment, along with the small coffee table and the plush-covered couch. A laptop, a portable CD player, and an MP3 player sat on the coffee table, and he saw a DVD player under the TV. Two built-in bookshelves were jammed with familiar titles he could imagine being *de facto* banned in a religious community—all seven *Harry*

Potter novels, several by Stephen King, some classic science fiction, Toni Morrison's *Song of Solomon*, *Women in Love*, *Catch-22*, *A Farewell to Arms, Gone With the Wind, To Kill a Mockingbird—*

"Forget the books," Camille said. "We're not searching for books." A number of DVDs were on the list, though, and she selected several from the shelf below the books.

Jesse went into the kitchen. Was it only last night when Sariah had asked if she should get a Keurig? Get, not buy. Another TV set was on the counter. She couldn't have stolen it—she didn't have a car—but who needed two TVs for one person? The microwave was a good one, a 1200-watt model with all the features. It might be Peggy's too. Sariah couldn't have taken it on the bus. Did shoplifters call for taxis? On the sink were an automatic soap dispenser and a couple of elegant vases with bouquets of silk flowers.

He opened a few drawers. The small items troubled him most. She had said she didn't cook now, but she possessed a set of tools and gadgets suitable for a gourmet chef. He couldn't even guess the use of some of them, but one appeared to be what his grandmother used to make flowers out of radishes. There were a lot of knives, all shiny and new-looking. Officer Diane Rosenberg, a motherly veteran cop with short, blonde hair, followed him in and pointed out items on the list. They carefully tagged and bagged them, and Jesse grew increasingly disoriented as he noted them on the inventory. This was Sariah's kitchen, not an abstract crime scene.

The pantry shelves held more canned goods than she could possibly need, although he understood

Mormons were advised to stockpile a year's supply of food. It was ordinary stuff, but Jesse wasn't familiar with some of the brands. She had stolen from the pet shop as well—bags of feed, toys, and water dishes, even though she didn't have a bird. The owner liked and trusted her. So had he.

"Aaron!" Camille called, and he went toward her voice. She was in the bedroom with Rosenberg's young partner, Officer Ibarra. The bedside table was also cluttered: a small lamp, a clock radio, two books—one was *Fifty Shades of Grey*—a mirrored tissue holder, an iPhone similar to the one she said she didn't know how to use, two decorative paperweights, and a large flashlight. Camille stood in front of the closet and pointed inside. Jesse sent Ibarra to help Rosenberg in the kitchen and joined her.

Whatever else she might have taken, Sariah's preference was obviously for handbags and shoes. He had seen two purses, but she had about fifteen, some with the price tags still attached, and dozens of pairs of shoes. The clothes racks were crowded with designer jeans and beautiful sweaters. Camille checked a few of the labels and said, "She has expensive tastes." She looked at him and nodded toward the dresser. "Try the jewelry box."

The top of the dresser was crowded—two cameras, several pairs of sunglasses, a two-shelf display rack containing fragile ceramic figurines, a tortoiseshell brush and comb set, several bottles of expensive perfume, and the large, three-tiered, walnut-finish jewelry box. Was she crazy? Peggy could easily have seen all of this.

Camille had another thought: "She must be good at

this, not to have been caught earlier."

The list included several items from Granger's Jewelry. He pulled open the top drawer of the box. There wasn't much in it, but everything looked expensive. He hoped it wasn't—the greater value could mean jail time. *I'm not a diamonds kind of girl.* The second drawer held a miscellaneous jumble, including several watches, and right on top were his silver cufflinks. Why would she want them? Some women wore cufflinks with tailored suits, but that wasn't her style. Maybe they had sentimental value—he could always claim he gave them to her. He and Camille were supposed to watch each other inventory each seized item, but he made sure her attention was elsewhere and put the cufflinks in his pocket.

When he was finished with the jewelry box he opened the dresser drawers. They were full of lacy underthings, not just the kind he had seen Sariah in—all kinds, in overwhelming abundance. The large Westfield mall included a Victoria's Secret, but he was only supposed to search for sweaters from Softwear.

"You pervert," Camille said.

When he finished with the drawers, he went into the bathroom. It was small, with a plain plastic shower curtain and a rag rug, but the counter was crowded with cosmetics and the medicine cabinet full of over-the-counter drugs. He couldn't detect a pattern to the medications—Advil, Claritin, Listerine, Benadryl, Mylanta, Pepto-Bismol, Zyrtec, Tylenol, Zantac, Motrin, Unisom, a few he didn't know the use of, in some cases two or three bottles of each, all apparently unopened.

"This's been going on for a *long* time," Camille

said from the doorway. The vanity drawer held antiseptic creams, lotions, sunscreen, Band-Aids, two electric shavers, and a gadget for "microdermabrasion," whatever that was—it was on the list. Sariah also had two brands of condoms, which she had little experience with, Plan B—the so-called morning-after pill—and three home pregnancy tests.

He felt as if his blood pressure was rising. "You were right," he said. "I shouldn't be here. I'll wait outside."

He sat in the car for about ten minutes before Peggy Dunwood emerged from her house and gestured for him to lower the window. "What is going on?" she asked. "It's my property. Don't I have a right to know?"

"We'll be glad to show you the warrant, but I can't comment on the case."

"You said Sariah was a witness. Did she do something wrong?"

"I can't comment—"

"Don't be so stuffy, Mister Detective."

"Detective Aaron."

"Why are you sitting out here, Mister Detective *Aaron*? Is this a stakeout?" she asked eagerly.

He had to smile. "No. I'm just goofing off."

"Well, come on in and goof off with me. Have a drink with me."

"Not while I'm—"

"On duty, I know." She sighed.

"It would be best if you wait inside," he said.

"Okay, but if you change your mind, ring the bell." She went in, and Jesse was alone again with his brutal thoughts.

Chapter Fifteen

By the time Jesse and Camille had returned the search warrant and inventory to the court and the judge had signed the arrest warrant, it was almost time for Sariah to get off work at World of Wings. Camille wanted Jesse to wait in the car again, but he couldn't pretend to be a disinterested spectator.

"Let me just ask her to come out here."

"Man up, Aaron. You need to stop protecting her."

"Please," he said and went to open the door. He didn't wait to see if she would follow, but she didn't. The owner was at the cash register completing a sale, while Sariah assisted another customer. "Sariah, I need to speak to you." She glanced at him, but continued with the customer. "Sariah!"

The owner thanked the young woman at the cash register and called to Jesse, "Hang on a minute—or I can help you."

He knew Camille was about to charge in and make a scene, so he said urgently, "Sariah, you need to come outside with me right now."

She looked at him blankly and then at the owner, who apologetically took over with the customer. Sariah followed him outside. "What's wrong?" she asked. Then she noticed Camille and the patrol car.

Officer Rosenberg did the honors: "Sariah Louise Brennan, you are under arrest for the crime of grand theft." She directed her to put her hands behind her back, handcuffed her with practiced ease, and patted her down.

Sariah met Jesse's eyes. He expected anger or an accusation of betrayal, but instead she looked only slightly embarrassed. "No flowers this time," she said.

****

"You have the right to remain silent," Camille began.

Sariah smiled faintly. It was not an uncommon response. People heard the familiar Miranda mantra all the time on TV, so it was like a joke when it was applied to them. He let Camille take the lead, but explained the process as much as he could. In the interrogation room, after they each signed the Waiver of Rights form, Camille gestured for Sariah to take a seat.

She didn't sit down. "I won't talk to you," she said. "I'll talk to Jesse."

"Detective Aaron," Camille said frostily.

Sariah flushed. "Detective Aaron," she echoed.

"Yeah, well, he doesn't get to question you, honey. It's gonna be me, whether you like it or not. You can be cooperative, or you can piss me off and do it the hard way." It was Camille at her most formidable.

"Why can't Jesse—Detective Aaron—"

Camille slammed her fist down on the table— which, after all, was where *he* had learned it. "Because he fucked you, that's why."

Sariah flinched—not at the blow, but at the word— and then rallied. "You used racial epithets toward me in front of a witness."

"I did no such thing."

"Honky. Skanky white something—I think I can remember the rest when you stop *leaning* on me." He knew where she had picked that up.

"Camille," Jesse said, half warning, half appeal. "Five minutes. Please."

She glared at them both and then went out and slammed the door hard.

Sariah sat down and looked up at him. "It wasn't *that*," she said fervently. He didn't know what she meant at first. "Except once. The other times were better than that...weren't they?"

"Yes," he said, but he kept his voice even. He reminded himself he was furious with her and sat down across from her. "Five minutes. Start talking."

"I don't know why I took those things," she said. "Some of them I couldn't even use. I never planned to steal anything. It just sort of happened."

"I don't care about the shoplifting," he said. "That's for Robbery." He didn't know when this had occurred to him: "Did you steal Kimberly Jackson's phone?"

Sariah bit her lip. "Yes. I didn't even know how to use it. I almost threw it out when I saw what was on it."

"And that was why you wouldn't let me see your apartment—because it was full of stolen goods?"

"No! I told you why."

"Did you witness Rosa Logan's murder?"

"No. They told me I couldn't come back to the shopping center. Do they have a right to keep me away?"

"Yes, they do. It's private property."

"So I wasn't supposed to be there, but I liked a lot of the stores. I needed to buy things, didn't I? *Shopping* isn't a crime."

"It's not the only mall in town."

"It's the easiest to get to on the bus, and it has stores the others don't."

"So you went to the shopping center? On the night of the murder? It was kind of late, wasn't it?"

"A lot of the stores are open late. I had…something. A security guard was watching me, and I wanted to get rid of it. It wasn't even from Plaza Center."

"Sariah—where is this headed?"

"Oh, you know. You were so sure all along. The back door of the warehouse was open, and a light was on inside. I didn't see what he did to her, but I saw him and all the blood, and he put her finger in his mouth. I couldn't be a witness. I couldn't be there. I kept seeing it in my head over and over. It was easy to make myself believe it was the only place I saw it. Not just to keep it from you—I didn't want to have seen it. I couldn't stand having seen it."

"And you knew him from before? Was he your fence?"

"What? Fence?" She was bewildered. "I didn't know him. I told you I didn't."

"Then how did you know his name?"

Camille rapped on the window. Had it been five minutes? He held up a hand to let her know Sariah was talking. "I didn't," Sariah said. "Just Casey."

"*How* did you know it was Casey? Did somebody say his name? Rosa? Or was somebody else there?"

"No. Rosa was dead. Nobody else was there. *I* wasn't there. How could I be? Maybe it was a dream. Maybe it *was* a vision."

"I don't think so. Did *he* see *you*?"

"No. He turned around, but he didn't look right at me."

"What about the night Elisabeth Wilson was attacked? Were you there?"

"Where?"

"The warehouse. Where else? What are we talking about?"

"No, of course I wasn't. I would never go there again."

"You didn't call me from the warehouse?"

"No." She shook her head emphatically. "Why would I be there?"

"Where were you? Where did you call from?"

"Home—the apartment. Didn't you recognize the number? Where I've been every night since it happened, except when I was with you."

"Then how did you know K.C. went to the warehouse?"

Sariah shrugged and looked out the window. Camille was at her desk, typing furiously on her computer, a deep scowl on her face. "She hates me," she said. "She probably hates every woman you get involved with. She's your work wife. Isn't that what they call it?"

"Never mind about Camille. How did you know K.C. was at the warehouse when Elisabeth Wilson was attacked?"

"I don't know. I just did. I called the hospital today, but they wouldn't tell me anything."

"I thought you said you didn't know her."

"I don't, but I can still care about her."

"You didn't seem very concerned about her

141

yesterday."

"I knew she would be all right as soon as I called you. Do you think she'll be able to tell you—?"

"Sariah! Don't get weird on me. Focus. How—did—you—know?"

"I don't know!" It was a shout of angry exasperation.

He took a deep breath and waited for her to calm herself. "Okay, let's go back. You saw K.C. in the warehouse, and then you saw Rosa Logan's picture in the paper and...?"

"At first they didn't print a picture or her name. It sounded like the right place, but I wasn't sure. Later, after she was identified or the next of kin notified or something, there *was* a picture, but she looked a lot different, so I still wasn't sure. And then I saw her name."

"And?"

"I knew the name. I heard the story—somewhere..."

"Focus. What story? What did you hear?"

"She was using the name Rosa Logan now and to be careful because Casey might come after her and Elisabeth, because he was very angry they left and had been known to be violent."

"'Had been known to be violent'?" The phrasing was oddly formal. "*Where* did you hear this?"

Her eyes were wide and dark—she was deciding again if she could trust him. "Okay," she said. "The organization that helped me relocate. I overheard something."

"How did you know Elisabeth was spelled with an s?"

"Oh." She considered. "I guess I didn't hear…No, I saw it written."

"Which is it? Are you making this up as you go along?"

"No!" Apparently the accusation stung, even though she had lied to him from the start. "I saw it written in a letter." He thought that was true—*had been known to be violent* sounded more like written language. "I wasn't supposed to see it. I wasn't supposed to be in the room."

"You were stealing something?" he suggested. "You were already stealing? Even from people who were helping you?" She didn't answer, but she didn't need to. She had a decidedly guilty flush. "Come on, would you believe this? You happened to witness, or almost witness, the murder of someone you happened to have heard or read about?"

"I don't know, but it's the truth."

"There has to be another connection." He leaned forward for emphasis. "Don't you see? We might have had a chance to stop him if you'd told us the truth. If we'd known Rosa Logan and Elisabeth Wilson were running from this Casey person, we could have gone to the organization for information on him."

"I didn't think they had any. If they did, they would have gone to the police."

"But it wasn't your call. If you'd just let me do my job…"

"You thought he was dead anyway."

"Sariah!"

"All right! I'm sorry. Are you happy? I should have told you I'd seen the letter."

"So…they were like you—polygamists?"

143

"I don't know. They do help other women, but maybe, because both of them were running from the same man. They weren't from Mackay."

"Rosa Logan's real name was Rosanna Milne. She was from Nevada. She filed an assault complaint, but withdrew it before an arrest was made. It could have been Casey under another name."

She stared. "How do you know that?"

"Let's see, I could claim I had a vision. How do you think I knew? I'm a detective. When people cooperate and tell me the truth, sometimes I find out things."

"I told you everything I could."

"You didn't tell me Elisabeth's name at first, even though you knew she was a potential victim."

"I didn't remember it at first. It was a long time ago."

"And again—how did you know he wouldn't pawn the ring?"

"I don't know. If he gave it to her, he would want it back—not sell it."

"How did you know he would be at the warehouse Sunday night?"

"I don't know."

"If you want me to believe you, you have to tell me everything."

"I did."

Stalemate. He would have to let Camille take a crack at her, although he wasn't convinced she would do better. He put down his pen and sat back in his chair. "Oh, Sariah," he said, a mournful whisper.

"I didn't have to come to you with this information at all, you know. I could have kept quiet, or I could have made an anonymous call."

"Why didn't you?"

"Would you have believed me? You didn't anyway, but if I hadn't looked at the pictures, you wouldn't have followed up on K.C.'s death certificate. If I told you I was an eyewitness I would have to testify under cross-examination, and they would try to find ways to discredit my testimony. I didn't think the prosecutor would risk putting a psychic on the stand. I did help you, in spite of your resistance, and you investigated *me*, and I'm the one who's in trouble."

"Yes, because you were doing something wrong, and you would have been caught sooner or later anyway. It was inevitable."

"What's going to happen to me?" she asked.

"Robbery will have some questions first, and then you'll go through the booking procedures. I'm afraid you'll have to spend tonight in jail. It can be unpleasant, but you're tough." He tried not to remember her at her most vulnerable. "Tomorrow you go to court for a bail hearing. After that, it's hard to tell. It's up to the judge. I think the total value is enough for a felony charge, which means jail time. Otherwise, for a first offense, it would probably be a fine, probation, and maybe community service. My advice? Full disclosure and restitution. Plead guilty to all the charges. Ask for a mental health evaluation. Listen to your lawyer. Don't make excuses. Be cooperative and contrite in court. If you haven't been in trouble before—"

"If?"

"Don't argue everything the way you do with me."

"I don't."

"By which you mean: Yes sir, Detective Aaron,

whatever you say. Repeat after me: Yes, sir."

"Yes, sir." She gave him a faint smile.

"Now." He tore a page from his notebook and laid it in front of her. "Write down the name of the organization that helped you. Names of people, address, phone number, e-mail, website, whatever you have." He handed her a pen.

"They won't…"

"What was that?"

"Yes, sir." She started writing. "What are you going to do?" she asked.

"Give it to Camille. I'm guessing they'll be more forthcoming with a woman."

"And it will give her something to do besides—"

"That too. Now, unless you want to continue to assist our investigation by telling me what you've held back, I'm going to hand you off to Robbery. They'll take you to Booking."

Everything that had happened between them was in her eyes. "Jesse, I—"

"Detective Aaron. Sir." He smiled to make light of the necessary formality.

She didn't smile back. "*Jesse*—I'm not holding back. I don't know how I knew, but I did."

"Uh-huh. You had a vision. You lied about having visions, and then you had a real one. How convenient." He stood up and took the piece of paper. She had written *Sisterhood League*, an 800 number, and an e-mail address. "How about the name of somebody there? Somebody you talked to?"

"They only gave first names. Some of them had been in abusive relationships."

"First names then. Come on."

She hesitated and then took the paper back to write *Inez* and *Nola.*

Jesse sat down again and folded the paper. "If you tell me how you knew Capek was at the warehouse, I'll speak to the DA and at your sentencing hearing. It's a good deal, Sariah. No matter what you tell me—unless you killed someone, and even then I would...try to help."

"And if I can't, you won't? I would give you what you want, even if it would be a lie, if I could think of one."

"All right," he said resignedly. "I'm sure Detective Farris will have a few more questions, but we're done here."

"Okay, K.C. was my—what do you call it? My fence—receiver of stolen property, right? I stole, he received. And I killed Rosa Logan, but I knew you would feel bad if you didn't save Elisabeth, so I let her live."

"You're lying."

"Of course I'm lying. It's what you wanted."

"All right." He got up again and started for the door.

"You won't help me? After what happened between us? It meant nothing to you?"

Jesse glanced through the window to see if Camille was watching before he took the few steps to where Sariah sat, looking up at him in tearful appeal. She put her arms around his waist and hid her face against his shirt. He held her close, but just for a moment, and then disentangled himself. Her warmth and softness had stirred an ache in his chest. "Sorry," he said and left her there.

He handed the folded paper to Camille. "This is an organization that helped Logan and Wilson relocate here. They were running from a guy named Casey."

She studied the neatly printed words. "Sisterhood?"

"It has other meanings. It's like a private WITSEC for women. They helped Brennan too, which is how she knew about Casey."

"That it?"

"She confessed to the murder of Rosa Logan."

"You're kidding."

"No, but she was. Apparently she did witness it—or the immediate aftermath—so her description is good. The not-as-dead-as-we-thought Kazimir Capek is Casey."

"No, wait a minute," Camille said. "These folks helped the victims relocate *here?* Capek lived here." It was so annoying when she did that—catching something he had stupidly overlooked.

"Lives," he said.

"Yeah, maybe. And *both* victims? Neither one could go to the police?"

"I think it was a domestic violence situation, and the local police weren't sympathetic. If they were polygamists…"

"Polygamy again. Honest to God, Aaron, haven't you ever seen a Mormon? They don't look like Kazimir Capek dead or alive or like Elisabeth Wilson."

"That's profiling. There are black Mormons—I've seen pictures. Anyway, Sa—Brennan said they aren't Mormons—the polygamists."

"Yeah, right." She dropped the paper on her desk and marched toward the interrogation room. Jesse opened his mouth to protest, but he had no legitimate grounds. He should have let her handle this to begin with.

She was inside for about ten minutes. He could hear her loud voice a few times, but not what she shouted. He tried not to feel sorry for Sariah. He should cut his losses and let her take the consequences, but he could at least tell the DA she had assisted in their investigation, and maybe Sex Crimes would do the same. Jesse put in a call and typed up his report to keep himself occupied.

Camille came out and slammed the door. "She's as useless as you are," she said. "I don't think she cares what happens to her."

"What did she say?"

"Nothing new. She knows better than to try her vision crap with me, but she won't give me a straight answer. Now she's invoking her right to remain silent." She snorted in disgust and picked up the phone.

Jesse couldn't resist one last look toward the interrogation room and then wished he hadn't. Sariah was sitting where he had left her, her head in her hands, and that was the way he would have to remember her—shamed, forsaken, and just barely penitent.

Chapter Sixteen

It was early the next day when the call came: Elisabeth Wilson's stolen Kia had been located. It was parked near the Bank of America in the Westfield shopping center. Camille was on the phone with an understandably cautious representative of the Sisterhood League, and Jesse gave her a sign his call was urgent and started for the elevator. Camille was right behind him.

"Get anything?" he asked.

"I'll call them back."

In the car on the way to the mall, Camille said, "I'm so hot for this guy, after dealing with this other crap. Nonviolent offenders are such a pain."

Jesse didn't answer, but a minute later he asked, "You ever see *The Maltese Falcon*?"

"Sure. Everybody's seen it. Bogey—very cool."

"Mary Astor, right? She's supposed to be the love interest, but she turns out to be the bad girl."

"And a consummate liar. Yeah. Sorry, Bogey." He figured that was the most sympathy he'd ever get from her.

The two patrolmen who spotted the car were in the shopping center parking lot, far enough away that they wouldn't be seen from the bank. They had the description of Kazimir Capek but hadn't gone into the bank to see if he was inside. After a brief discussion, they decided Jesse would be the best bet to go in, because he looked less like a cop than Camille. He wasn't sure it was a compliment.

He could see at a glance as he entered that Capek was not there. The car thief—and indeed the assailant—could be somebody else. They had only Sariah's dubious identification in favor of his involvement. "Hey," he called casually. "Anybody belong to the blue Kia? I accidentally scraped the door."

The bank customers and staff stared at him blankly. A few voices chorused, "No." Nobody was hesitant, concerned, or shifty-eyed.

"Okay, thanks," he said and left. He shook his head for the benefit of Camille and the patrol officers and surveyed the immediate area. The bank was one of several businesses located on the perimeter of the parking lot, with the majority of the shops grouped around a central courtyard on the other side. The mall had enough available parking, so the drivers of cars parked here could be assumed to be patronizing one of the street-side businesses—the bank, the Perennial Garden Center, the CVS Pharmacy, or the Outback Steakhouse. The restaurant wasn't open until four, and the other two would be harder to search than the bank.

He went back to the car. The CVS had more aisles than the open-plan garden center, so the uniformed patrol officers took it, and Camille went to the garden center. Jesse went back to the bank and asked to speak to the manager. He wanted to know if any of the employees had noticed how long the car had been parked in front—no—and he wanted to see the security tapes. Unfortunately, the camera on the parking lot had been reset before the bank opened Monday morning, and the blue car was already there. He also showed them Capek's mug shot, but nobody recognized him.

Within twenty minutes, they were reasonably sure the stolen Kia had been abandoned and had it towed to the crime lab garage to be searched. Elisabeth Wilson's insurance card and registration were in the glove compartment along with the owner's manual, a pen, a pack of Wet Ones wipes, and a map of California. The interior was clean enough—not a hair or fiber to be found—to suggest the thief had vacuumed it.

Fingerprints showed up in all the logical places, mostly blurred partials, which would probably prove to be Wilson's. The trunk held the spare tire, a scissor jack, and a reusable TruMart bag full of groceries. The receipt inside was from the Self Checkout and listed the time as 9:13 p.m. It gave the name of the manager, but not the address of the store. The groceries included a carton of frozen yogurt, which was now melted to slush and had leaked into the bag. The rest was ordinary: Honey Nut Cheerios, rice, spaghetti, canned soups, tuna, a loaf of bread, and a jar of Postum. "I thought this stuff had been discontinued," the crime lab tech commented. Jesse agreed—but hadn't he seen it somewhere else in the last few days? Maybe it was *déjà vu.*

****

Camille had been unable to get any information from the Sisterhood League on the phone, but was given the number of the local contact and made an appointment to talk to her. They decided they would go together, but Jesse would leave if the woman was uncomfortable in his presence. The idea that he might be considered more threatening than Camille was almost comforting in his present mood.

The address they were given proved to be a private home on a quiet residential street along the edge of a canyon. It was a modest bungalow with an untidy flower garden and a small, green lawn. Camille rang the bell, and the door was opened almost at once by a young white boy. At first Jesse guessed he was about twelve, but then realized he was older, perhaps late teens, with the distinctive appearance of Down syndrome. He wore blue jeans and a neon green T-shirt emblazoned with a colorful zombie image. "Hi," Camille said with uncharacteristic gentleness—she could be kind when she tried, especially with children. "We're here to see Mrs. Maxwell."

"Grandma!" the boy hollered, and then he grinned at them and turned away.

The woman who came to the door next was tiny and plump, with snow-white hair. She peered up at them through granny glasses and said, "Oh, my goodness. You're so official," and to Camille, half apologetic, half admiring, "You sounded so sweet on the phone. Detective Farris?"

Camille showed her badge. "And Detective Aaron," she said.

"Jesse," he said, struggling to keep a straight face. *Sweet?* Camille gave him a look, as if she thought he was flirting.

"Olivia Maxwell," the white-haired woman said, "but everybody calls me Maxie. Aaron like Hank Aaron, right? Do you follow baseball at all? It's the one sport I *get*, you know, takes real skill." She opened the door and ushered them in. "Everything's fine, Troy," she said to the boy, who stood watchfully in a doorway.

"Go on in." He disappeared. "He's very protective," she told them in a stage whisper. She led them into what could only be called a parlor, comfortable and old-fashioned, with an overstuffed couch and easy chairs. The room smelled of furniture polish and citrus air freshener. A Yorkshire terrier was perched on one of the chairs. It regarded them with mute curiosity but didn't move. "Rest yourselves," Mrs. Maxwell said. It was a phrase Jesse had never heard before from a white person or from anyone younger than his grandmother. He didn't think Camille liked it, but she sat down on the couch without comment, and he joined her.

"Mrs. Maxwell," she began.

"Maxie, please. Can I get you folks anything to drink? I have some lemonade or oh, gosh, cherry pop?"

Jesse again had trouble keeping a straight face, and Camille was speechless. "No, thanks," he answered for both of them.

"Do you think it will rain again?" Mrs. Maxwell asked. "We could sure use some."

"Hard to tell," Jesse said. He felt Camille tense, about to be rude, and said, "We were given your name as a contact for the Sisterhood League?"

"That's right." She became all business. "We don't like to have the police involved. We encourage the ladies to go to the police if need be, but usually they need more discreet help, if you know what I mean." She picked up the fluffy Yorkie and sat down with it in her lap.

"We expected an office," Camille said.

Mrs. Maxwell smiled. "We do have offices, but it's more of a network."

"So I guess you wouldn't have files on the women

you've helped?"

"Of course we do. It's the new millennium, Detective Farris. Information at your fingertips. Thing is, it's all confidential. The ladies need privacy. They need to trust us."

Undeterred, Camille showed her the photos of Rosa Logan and Elisabeth Wilson. "Do you recognize these women?"

Mrs. Maxwell stroked the dog and leaned forward to peer at the pictures. "Oh, sure," she said comfortably and sat back.

"What can you tell us about them?" Camille prompted.

"Not a thing."

Camille held up Rosa's picture again. "This one is dead," she said.

"Yes…it was in the paper. It was a dreadful shock. Don't you think if we had any information that would help solve her murder, we would have passed it on?"

"You can't always know what would help," Jesse told her. "That's our job. If she was killed by someone from her past—"

"She wasn't," Mrs. Maxwell said. "The whole point was to sever the ties to her past life, for her protection."

Camille held up the second photo. "This one is in the hospital," she said. "She was brutally attacked in the same place in the same way. You think it's a coincidence? You help these women relocate here, and they end up dead?"

Mrs. Maxwell stopped stroking the dog. "Liz was attacked?"

"Her throat was cut," Jesse said. "She may not

survive. We haven't found any connection between them in their new lives, but maybe they had one in the past? Even in federal witness protection, sometimes people are tracked down."

Seconds ticked by in silence while Mrs. Maxwell stared at them. She sighed deeply and handed Camille the dog. "It will take a few minutes to access and print out the files," she said. She got up and then added to Camille, "For your eyes only. Just you," and to Jesse, "Nothing personal. We don't think all men are the enemy or anything, but we are a *sister*hood."

Camille held the Yorkie awkwardly, almost at arm's length. Jesse laughed and took it from her. He wasn't fond of small, yippy breeds, but this one was very mellow, perhaps as old in dog years as its mistress. He was content to hold it on his lap and scratch its ears while they waited. Camille gestured toward the hall door where the grandson now stood watching them.

"Hi," Jesse said casually. "Troy, right?"

"Yes, sir. That's my dog," he added. "His name is Weinerschnitzel."

Camille laughed and then said apologetically, "It's a funny name."

"Yes, ma'am, it is. It's a joke, because he's not a wiener dog."

"Very clever," she said. "Did you name him?"

"Yup," Troy said, forgetting his company manners. "I'm very 'maginative."

"Good for you," she said. "Imagination will take you a long way."

"Do you go to school?" It was all Jesse could think of to ask.

"Well, duh," was the reply. Troy and Camille

exchanged a longsuffering look.

Mrs. Maxwell came to his rescue. "You entertaining our guests?" she asked. "Thanks, baby. I'll take it from here."

"I'm not a baby," he said.

"I know, I know," she said and gave him an affectionate pat to send him on his way. She held up two manila folders, carefully out of Jesse's reach. To Camille she said, "I'd better see your badge again, dear." She complied, and Mrs. Maxwell pushed her glasses up her nose to peer at her ID. "Camille," she said approvingly. "Such a lovely name."

****

Camille laid a sheet of paper on Jesse's desk. "That look like the letter your girl saw?" she asked. It was a copy of an e-mail addressed to Maxie and signed Inez. He skimmed through chatty generalities to find the crucial lines:

R will show up on your doorstep probably Thursday night. She will be using the name Rosa Logan. Please be particularly careful on this one, as with Elisabeth, because the husband will be very angry and has been known to be violent. We don't want another Casey incident.

It wasn't exactly what Sariah had remembered, but if it was several months ago, and she hadn't expected it to be important, she had done pretty well. She couldn't have known how much difference it might have made if she had been more forthcoming in the beginning.

Camille was waiting. "It doesn't say Casey was the husband," she pointed out.

"No, but you can see why Brennan assumed he was. It doesn't say Wilson was running from the same

157

guy, either."

"But in fact," Camille said, brandishing another page, "she was. His name is Udell Jorgensen. He was born in a Mormon Fundamentalist community, but kicked out—one of the 'lost boys' as they call them."

"You did your homework."

"Yeah, and that *is* a cult, if you ask me. So anyway, he married both Logan and Wilson—AKA Abigail Evans—and did not treat them very well, so they split. Separately, about a year apart. They were both relocated to Carroll City but were not given each other's new information."

"So who is Casey?"

"He's not mentioned anywhere else in either file. Jorgensen doesn't match the description—he's your basic boring, blond Mormon type. Still lives in Utah. We should have the local police question him. It's not as if we can trust Brennan's description."

Jesse let the remark pass, although the DNA wouldn't match either. "So it's back to Mrs. Maxwell," he said. "*She* knows who Casey is."

****

"It was a long time ago," Mrs. Maxwell said, "but it haunts us."

"How long ago?" Jesse asked.

"Oh, Lord." She stroked Weinerschnitzel and considered the question. "Five, six years maybe. Someone we no longer work with inadvertently released some information. We're a lot more savvy about online security now." It occurred to him their security might still be suspect, if they let Sariah see a confidential document, but he kept his mouth shut. "One of our ladies was snatched right off the street and taken back to her abusive husband," Mrs. Maxwell said. "We didn't know what had happened for a long time. She just disappeared. Then she contacted us again. Her husband hired a kind of bounty hunter to track her down and take her back. Casey was the only name she knew him by. He was very brutal about it—the abduction. Hit her on the head and tied her up and threw her in the trunk of his car. Drove her straight back to Utah without even a bathroom break, hauled her out of the trunk, and dumped her on the ground in front of her husband."

"And this was never reported to the police?" Camille asked.

"Oh, yes, we made a missing persons report at the time, but there were no witnesses to the kidnapping. We didn't know about this bounty hunter person until she got away again."

"It would have helped to know about it then," Camille said sternly. "Now he's graduated to murder."

"Oh, no, no," Mrs. Maxwell said, shaking her head vigorously. "It wasn't Casey—whoever it was, it wasn't him."

"How do you know?" Jesse asked.

"Casey's dead. Somebody sent her his obituary. That's why she got up the nerve to try again."

"Somebody?" Camille asked.

"Yes, it was anonymous."

"Who would have sent it?" Camille turned to Jesse, puzzled. "Somebody who knew…?"

"Or he did it himself," he suggested. "The obituary would have given his full name," he pointed out.

"I suppose so. It had his picture, so she knew it was him."

"And…what was the name?"

"I have no idea. I don't think anybody asked her. He was dead, after all."

"He faked his death," Camille said starkly. "He killed Rosa or Rosanna or whatever you want to call her."

"Oh, my," was all Olivia Maxwell had to say.

Camille, at her formidable best, demanded the name of the woman who had been kidnapped and her husband. She should be contacted and warned, and if they could get a statement from her and have her look at mug shots, they might be one step closer to finding Casey. Even better, her husband might know how to contact him—if he would cooperate.

Meekly, Mrs. Maxwell explained that she didn't have immediate access to the information, but promised to contact someone in the Sisterhood League who would, and let them know.

"In the meantime," Camille said as they left, "we have exactly nothing to go on. This case is nothing but dead ends."

Chapter Seventeen

A memory surfaced in the middle of the night—where else he had seen a jar of Postum. In Sariah's pantry. Jesse had thought it was a relic of the past, along with rabbit ears and decoder rings. Out of idle curiosity rather than the hope of finding a connection, he went online to check it out. It hadn't been discontinued until 2007, and it was revived by another company in 2012. As a coffee substitute, it was popular with members of the LDS church. It was primarily sold online, but the product's official website included a store locator. It was not sold at TruMart. Nearly all of the retail outlets listed were in the Smiths Food and Drug chain in Utah, Nevada, and Arizona. He didn't think Smiths even existed in California. He put his own zip code in the search box, and the nearest location was given as Hearty Natural Foods in the Plaza Center shopping mall.

He put the store on his to-do list for the morning, but before he could head for the mall, the long-awaited call came—Elisabeth Wilson was awake and able to talk. Camille was in the middle of an interview on another case, so he went alone. It was a heady sensation, being so close to some real answers for a change.

A male nurse warned him not to tire the patient and opened the door to the semi-private room where she lay flat in a narrow hospital bed. It would have been an understatement to say she looked much better than the last time Jesse had seen her, but she was still weak and ill. Her throat was wrapped in bandages, and she was hooked up to IVs and a heart monitor that emitted low, regular beeps.

"Ms. Wilson?" he said tentatively. He remained standing so she wouldn't have to turn her head.

She looked up at him and whispered a barely audible, "Yes."

He showed her his badge. "My name is Jesse Aaron. I'm a detective with the Carroll City Police Department."

Awareness sparked in her eyes—she recognized his name. "Saved my life," she said. It was louder this time, her voice painfully hoarse.

"I'm glad I could help," he said. "We'd like to find the person who did this to you. What can you tell us about him? Did you know him?"

Her head barely moved in negation, and it looked more painful than speech. "I don't know what happened," she whispered.

"Somebody hurt you, obviously. What do you remember about the night you were attacked?"

"Nothing… Sorry."

"It's okay. Sometimes details come back later. What's the last thing you remember?"

She looked at him helplessly. "I don't know."

"Your car was found a long way from where you were hurt. Do you remember driving it anywhere?"

"When?"

"That night or any time before?"

She shrugged slightly, which was also painful.

"What night?" she asked.

"The night you were hurt. Oh, sorry, Sunday, March second or very early the third." She looked confused. "We found groceries in your car. You went to TruMart on Sunday. Do you remember going to Plaza Center?"

She started to speak and then hesitated. "No," she said finally.

"Listen, if it hurts to talk, we could try blink once for no, twice for yes."

The suggestion amused her. "I can talk," she said.

"I appreciate your making the effort. I'd like to show you some pictures. Tell me if you know anyone or if anything about any of them is familiar." He held up three mug shots, one at a time. Nothing. She had said she had no conscious memory of the attack, but he hoped for an instinctive fight-or-flight response. No— not a flicker.

He took another tack. He held up the picture of Rosa Logan. Her eyes widened. "Ms. Wilson, we know about your previous life and how the Sisterhood League helped you. You know who this is, don't you?"

She took a few seconds before she whispered, "My sister wife."

"Did you know she was dead?"

"Yes."

"It's possible she was murdered by the same person who attacked you. We want to keep your secret, but it's possible someone from your past was behind this. Do you think…?"

"Udell?" she said harshly. It sounded so angry and panicked that he had to remind himself she was not in control of the tenor of her voice. "Is he here?"

"No, no, he isn't here, and he appears to have an alibi, but he might have hired someone. Do you think he would do that?" She seemed so overwhelmed that he held up a hand. "I'm sorry. I shouldn't tire you with so many questions."

"I just...don't remember."

"It's perfectly all right. I'll leave my card here on the table. If you start to remember, you can call or have someone call for you, and I'll come by again. Would that be all right?"

She nodded. He started to go, and she said, "Detective..."

"Yes?"

"I'm sorry. I forgot your name."

"Detective Aaron. Jesse."

"Jesse...Thank you. For saving me." Her voice broke, and grateful tears stood in her eyes.

"Uh, yeah. Glad to help. If I'd been faster, you wouldn't have been hurt at all."

He called Camille. She was disappointed, but agreed the memories might resurface. "Did you ask if she'd had consensual sex?" she asked.

"Camille, she doesn't remember the whole day, maybe more."

"Yeah, yeah. I hate fucking rapists. Are you on your way back?"

"I'm going to check out the TruMart at Plaza Center. She had Postum, which is sold at a health food store there. She might be on their security cameras."

****

The Plaza Center TruMart confirmed that Elisabeth Wilson had used their store. They kept their security recordings for a week and with the time on the receipt were able to zero in on her image. She had put her groceries in the trunk and driven away without incident. She appeared to be headed farther into the mall parking lot, not out to the street.

Hearty Natural Foods wasn't very big and didn't have security cameras. It faced on the plaza rather than the parking lot and had no dedicated parking spaces. Jesse spotted one customer inside, browsing in the back. The twenty-something clerk who manned the register went wide-eyed at the sight of the badge. "Wow!" he said.

"Detective Aaron."

"Am I like in trouble?"

"Not that I know of. Should you be?"

"Uh, no, I don't think so. Not sure what happened last Saturday night, though."

"I hope it was fun. I'm investigating a homicide and an attempted homicide."

"Like murder? Cool."

"Do you ever work in the evenings?"

"Yes, two to ten, two nights a week. We're open until ten, mainly because the Y has late yoga classes, and those are like our best customers."

"You sell Postum, don't you?"

"What? Oh, yeah, we do. It's like right over there." He pointed.

"I don't want to buy any, thanks. You sell a lot?"

"Not a lot, and mostly to the same few ladies."

"Ladies?"

"Yeah, it's not much of a guy thing. Couple older ladies and young ones who are like…"

"What?"

"I don't know, dress kind of square? Postum's like

an old-timey thing. It's good for you, though. Everything we sell here is good for you. Healthy. Natural. No junk food."

"I'm glad to hear it. Do you recognize any of these women?" Jesse laid five pictures out on the counter.

The clerk studied them with intent interest. "This one, yeah." He indicated Rosa Logan. "Nice lady, pretty too. Haven't seen her lately. Or this one— something hinky about her, not sure what." It was Sariah's picture. This was one of the stores she had taken the bus here for, one the other shopping malls didn't have. The young man hesitated over the other pictures. "I don't know about this one. There is a black girl who buys Postum, but I'm not sure this is her. I don't mean like you guys all look alike or anything— except, you know, I read this article where it's hardwired in your brain? It being easier to identify faces of your own race?…Sorry, never mind."

"Do you remember who bought Postum most recently?"

"Uh…when I was on?…I don't know." He closed his eyes in concentration. "I think it was the black girl. Sunday night, I think. Postum and…that might have been it. Said she didn't need a bag. Said good night, real nice." He opened his eyes and grinned, pleased with his recall.

Jesse laid three more pictures on the counter. "How about these?"

"This is so cool. Oh, I know this one. He buys vitamins and nutrition bars, but sometimes he's just like *here*, you know? He browses, and he watches the girls. Creepy." It was Kazimir Capek.

"When was he here last? Do you remember?"

"I don't know. Last week maybe. Don't know these other guys, but they wouldn't like stand out."

Jesse gathered up the pictures. "Thank you…" He glanced at the young man's name tag. "Thanks, Zack." He handed him a card. "If you see the creepy dude again, would you give me a call?"

"Uh, sure."

"I'd appreciate it."

"Hey, man," Zack called as he went out. "Who got murdered?"

Jesse didn't answer. He was still processing this information, suppressing his excitement. This was how Capek had found his victims. Had Udell Jorgensen hired him, or did he target Mormon Fundamentalist girls at random? Would Sariah have been next? In any case, here was the other connection he had known must exist. She was not Capek's fence or posing as his wife. She and Logan simply patronized the same store, possibly even on the same night, the night of the murder. This was why she had happened to be a witness. Perhaps the Sisterhood League had even told them both where to find Postum, whereas WITSEC would have advised them not to call attention to themselves by buying it.

Here also was a possible explanation for Sariah's knowledge that Capek was at the warehouse the night Elisabeth Wilson was attacked: she could have followed him from the health food store. Zack said she hadn't been there lately, but she could have seen Capek leaving and not gone in. But she should have called when she first saw him. He reminded himself she didn't carry a cell phone and it might have taken a while to find a landline she could use. But how could she have known he was headed for the warehouse? She couldn't have followed on foot, if he was in Wilson's car. It was still a puzzle.

He headed for the parking lot and then stopped to look back. The health food store was right next to a large Barnes & Noble with two entrances. One faced the plaza, and the main entrance opened onto the parking lot.

He went in, showed his badge to the nearest employee, and asked for the manager. As at TruMart, the bookstore's security cameras were computerized, and the manager was able to quickly call up the recording for Sunday night after nine o'clock. And there it was: a clearly visible abduction and carjacking.

A big, dark man—precisely Sariah's first description—approached a young woman as she closed her car's trunk. He struck her on the back of the head, and she staggered but didn't fall. He dragged her toward the front door on the passenger side. She appeared to be conscious, but unable to offer much resistance. He shoved her into the front seat, went around to get in on the driver's side, and drove away in a hurry.

Jesse couldn't positively identify either of them, but the license plate matched Wilson's. "Again," he said. On the second viewing, he could see that whatever the perp had used to hit Elisabeth with was still in his hand, pressed against her side, as he took her around the car—a gun or maybe a club or blackjack she might think was a gun, if she wasn't too stunned to think at all. "Again." The trunk wasn't quite closed, and he shoved the door down and took the keys out of her hand. Elisabeth's clothes looked like the ones Jesse had seen her in at the crime scene, with a scarf covering her hair. The perp was all in black, and yes, his profile was at least suggestive of Kazimir Capek's facial type.

Jesse called Camille. "It's about time we made some progress on this," she said.

"He drove her car from here to the warehouse and abandoned it in the other shopping center—so where was *his* car?" he asked. "If he left it here and came back for it, it would have been here for a while. It should also have been here and in the vicinity of the warehouse the night Rosa Logan was killed. He didn't carjack *her*. If he took a bus or taxi to Plaza Center when he took Wilson, he might have left his car at Westfield."

"So…what? Might show up on license plate scanners from routine patrols on those nights?"

"Great minds think alike. If we compare them…"

The partnership was back on track.

Chapter Eighteen

Jesse and Camille began the time-consuming job of searching through lists compiled by the computer, checking the DMV records of drivers whose cars had been scanned in one or more of the target locations on the nights of the crimes. Any hope of an easy solution soon faded. No driver's photo matched Casey's description. The only scanned car reported stolen had been recovered with the joyriding teenage thieves still on board. They kept at it for the rest of the day and started again the next morning.

The first break came when Camille noticed that a red 2012 Toyota Camry scanned in Plaza Center on February fifth and on a nearby street on March second was registered to a driver who had received a red-light-camera ticket on Meridian Avenue the previous June. Holy Cross Hospital was on Meridian.

Benjamin Franklin Daugherty was thirty and had a good DMV record with one other citation—overtime on a parking meter. He was a good-looking, husky young man with dark, reddish hair and glasses. His police record proved to be not as clean as his driving record—he had been convicted twice of selling Vicodin and Percocet. The first offense had led to a fine and probation, and he was currently incarcerated at the Twin Hills Correctional Facility on the second charge. He had been locked up for six months, so someone else had driven his car on February fifth and March second.

Jesse called the phone number for his last known address, but the new tenants didn't have any information about him. He spoke to the landlord, who remembered Daugherty's arrest and believed he had lived in the apartment alone. "Not married as far as I know," he said. "Don't think I ever saw a girlfriend with him. Kind of a loner, I guess."

"Do you know what happened to his car?"

"I wouldn't know. We don't have assigned parking spaces. I know there isn't a car that's been sitting here for six months."

"How about employment? Do you know where he worked before he was arrested?"

"It was a hospital; I remember that. He wasn't a doctor, maybe an orderly or clerk or something. Ben paid his rent, which was all I cared about."

"Do you know what hospital?"

"Don't remember if he ever said."

"Could it have been Holy Cross?"

"I don't know. It doesn't sound familiar, but I don't know if he said. Not my business, as long as the rent got paid, know what I mean?"

"It's thin," Camille said, "but if he was a records clerk, maybe he helped Capek fake the death certificate."

Jesse picked up the phone again. "He was on probation—his probation officer would have his employment records."

"Here's a car at both Plaza Center and Westfield on March second," Camille said. "If he had an accomplice, he or she could have driven his car from one to the other and picked him up after he abandoned Wilson's car."

"Worth checking out," he agreed.

Ben Daugherty's probation officer, John Hamaya, was apologetic about having to call them back, pleading his heavy workload. While they waited, Jesse and Camille made calls to track down Garry Underhill, whose car had been seen in both shopping centers. He was elusive enough to be a promising suspect.

Hamaya called back. "Detective Aaron—Ben Daugherty—Holy Cross Hospital—Five years—Need anything else?" He was clearly a busy man.

Jesse checked with the Holy Cross administration office. The same gravelly-voiced clerk who had answered the first time reported that Daugherty had worked as a clerk-typist in Medical Records for five years and had received satisfactory performance reports. He was quiet, well liked, and had never been accused of any wrongdoing on the job. His employment had understandably been terminated when he was arrested on drug charges.

Next stop: Twin Hills Correctional Facility.

They met in the smaller of the prison's visiting rooms, otherwise empty because it was not a normal visiting day. The clang of steel doors echoed in the silence before a guard ushered in the prisoner. Ben Daugherty had changed a bit since his DMV photo was taken. His hair was cut very short, and he looked older and tougher. He had gone into what Jesse recognized as survival mode.

"What the fuck's this about?" he asked. "I'm already doing the time."

"This is about your car, Mr. Daugherty. Do you know where it is?"

"My *car*? I'm in prison, man. I'm not doing a lot of driving, y'know?"

"I'm aware of that, thank you. Do you know where it is? Could it have been stolen? Did you give it to somebody, give somebody the keys?"

"Yeah, I gave the keys to a friend so he could move it, and he said he'd drive it now and then to keep the battery charged."

"Who's your friend?"

"Who the fuck cares? My friend, my car. Are you saying he let it get stolen?"

"Who's your friend?" Jesse repeated.

"I'll tell you his name when you tell me how it's your business."

"It may have been used in a crime."

"No, I don't think so. It's sitting in a garage."

"What garage?"

"I don't know. I don't think he said. Come on, what's this about?"

Jesse laid Kazimir Capek's mug shot on the small table between them.

"Shit," Daugherty said.

"This your boyfriend?"

"Don't say stuff like that in here, man! He's just a friend, not even a close friend. If he says I did anything with him, he's lying. If he committed a crime using *my* car, I don't know anything about it."

"But this is him? The guy you gave your car keys to?"

"Yeah. I said he could use it if he wanted. I owed him money. What did he say about me?"

"I haven't spoken to him. We don't have his current address. Do you?"

"I ain't gonna help you find him. I didn't think he was dealing. Was that it?"

"Did you help him fake his death?"

"Oh, fuck, man! I'm not gonna do any more time." Daugherty ran a hand over his close-cropped hair, his mouth a grim line.

"If you tell me the name he's using and where I can find him, I'll make sure you aren't charged with falsifying a death certificate."

"Yeah? You gonna put it in writing?"

"If you like."

"Really?" Daugherty probably knew it would be the DA's call whether to prosecute and Jesse's promise might be worthless. He hesitated. "What did he do?" he asked.

"Murder, kidnapping, carjacking, rape, and attempted murder."

"Shit! This guy?" He put his hand on the mug shot. "I knew he didn't like women much, but... Man, if this is a trick—"

"No trick, Mr. Daugherty. We need to find him."

Daugherty hesitated for another minute. Jesse let him think about it. "Okay," he said. "He called himself Casey Kovar. When I knew him he lived at the Pickett Hotel downtown. He wasn't around a lot because he spent most of his time in Utah. I don't know what he had going there."

"Did you know his wife?"

"His *wife*?"

"Mrs. Capek. She was collecting on his life insurance."

"I never heard about any wife. He said he had to fake his death because some guys were after him, like

Russian mobsters or something. Don't tell me it was an insurance scam."

"I'm afraid so," Jesse said. "As far as you know, he's still at the Pickett Hotel? Or in Utah?"

"I don't know, man. It's not like he writes me letters or shows up on visiting days."

"Do you know what kind of car he drives? His wife sold the one registered under his former name."

"I don't know. It was a Jeep Cherokee or something like that."

"Remember any part of the license plate?"

"No, why would I? I only saw it a couple times…It had Utah plates, I think."

****

As soon as he got his cell phone back at the gate, Jesse called Camille. "Jackpot," he said. "You can stop looking; Capek was using Daugherty's car. He was living at the Pickett Hotel under the name Casey Kovar."

She didn't waste any time. "K-o-v-a-r? I'll get the warrant in both names."

"We should try to get a search warrant as well—to look for Logan's ring."

"My theory is your klepto girlfriend has it."

"Don't, Camille. He might have Wilson's purse too, not to mention the murder weapon, but we'd better find out if he's still at the Pickett first. I'll call them and put out BOLOs for Daugherty's car and a Jeep Cherokee with Utah plates. That's what he was driving six months ago."

Camille sighed. "We *are* a good team—when you're not distracted."

****

The Pickett was an affordable residential hotel on a busy street of restaurants and bars. The tenants were a mixture of young professionals saving to buy homes and folks on the verge of homelessness. Jesse had been inside twice, and his strongest memory was of the vague odor of marijuana smoke in the halls. As a rookie patrol officer he had responded to a domestic violence call and as a homicide detective to a suspicious death, which had been ruled an accident.

He didn't identify himself on the phone as a police officer, and the desk clerk confirmed Casey Kovar's registration and gave Jesse the room number. Kovar probably wouldn't be home, but at least they had an address for the warrants.

He also contacted the Utah DMV and confirmed that a silver 2001 Jeep Cherokee was registered to Casey Peter Kovar. He updated the BOLO and passed the information on to Camille. The address on the Utah driver's license was in Richfield, and he sent a request for the local police to try to serve an arrest warrant.

Waiting was the hardest part of the job. Jesse started to get an edgy, anxious feeling in anticipation of the end of the hunt. He made sure all the paperwork was up-to-date and accurate, so no technicalities could trip them up in court. He tried not to think too much about the things that tried to weigh him down—with Sariah at the top of the list.

It was late afternoon when Camille called to say she had obtained an arrest warrant and search warrants for the Pickett Hotel, Ben Daugherty's car, and Kovar's Cherokee. Jesse was anxious to go downtown, but they had until ten p.m. to serve the search warrant, and another call intervened: A citizen had found a body in her swimming pool.

The homeowner was understandably distraught, and the patrol officers were trying to comfort her when Jesse and Camille arrived. The body was a Caucasian male, an older man judging by the age spots and weathered skin. The EMTs had confirmed he had been dead for hours and left the body where it was. It looked like an accidental drowning, but they would have to wait for the medical examiner to be sure. "How did he get in?" Jesse asked. The pool was in a fenced backyard.

Camille checked the gate, which was securely locked. The homeowner had been in the house for about an hour before she went out to the pool. She was dressed for a swim, in a stylish and skimpy bikini. She had put a wrap on over it, but it was flimsy, almost transparent material. Jesse didn't give undue attention to these details, but anything could be relevant at a possible crime scene.

Camille didn't see it that way. She nudged him in the ribs. "Wrong body," she said. "Mrs. Greenway? Do you know this gentleman?"

Mrs. Greenway stared at her. "No," she said and then admitted, "I couldn't look."

"Could you now, please?"

Mrs. Greenway peered at the form floating face down in the pool. "I can't see his face," she said.

"When the M.E. gets here, you can try again to identify him, but does the body or clothing look familiar?"

"N-no." She hid her face behind her hands, and one of the patrolmen patted her shoulder in a clumsy attempt to comfort her.

"Could he have come in through the house?" Jesse asked. "Was the door locked when you got home?"

Mrs. Greenway uncovered her face and blinked at him. "Yes, of course," she said tearfully. "I didn't notice anything unusual until I came out here."

Jesse nodded to one of the patrol officers. "Check the windows." While he did so, Jesse studied the body again. Muddy stains showed on the shoes and pants, and the shirt was torn. He pointed the signs out to Camille. "He may have climbed over the fence."

"Why does some old geezer scale a six-foot fence and go for a swim fully clothed?"

It didn't remain a mystery for long. When the medical examiner arrived, they were able to match the dead man's description to an elderly Alzheimer's patient who had been reported missing the day before. It was a sad ending to a life, but it was not a homicide.

****

The desk clerk at the Pickett Hotel was a Latina in her early thirties. She was perched on a stool watching the news on a small TV above the desk. She got up when Jesse and Camille approached and stood awkwardly with one hand on the small of her back. She looked tired, bored, and about eight months pregnant.

They showed her their badges and Capek's mug shot. "Do you know this individual?" Camille asked.

"I know he's rude," she said. "What did he do?"

"Is he in, do you know?" Jesse asked.

"No. I mean he could be, but I haven't seen him today. Or for a while, I guess. He goes out of town a lot—his mail piles up."

"Do you have anything for him now?" Camille asked.

She checked. "He hasn't picked it up today, but it's just a few ads and a catalog."

Camille showed her the search warrant. "We need somebody with a key in case he's not home."

"Okay." She picked up the phone. "Nancy? There's cops with a warrant down here…No, Mr. Kovar's room…They didn't say." She pointed to the elevator and mouthed, "Three twenty-one." She apparently wanted to continue her conversation in private, but they waited until she hung up.

"If you see Mr. Kovar come in," Jesse said, "call the room right away. Don't tell him we're here."

Her eyes widened. "Uh, sure." As they walked away, she repeated, "What did he do?"

The third floor hallway still smelled like marijuana. Nancy, a chubby, fortyish blonde, met them at the elevator. She was dressed in a white maid's uniform and pushing a cleaning cart. Camille put a finger to her lips, showed Nancy her badge, and gestured for her to precede them down the hall. At the door of Room 321, Camille gave her a nod, and Nancy knocked briskly. "Housekeeping," she called.

No answer. Camille motioned for Nancy to back away, repeated the knock, and announced, "Carroll City Police Department. We have a warrant to search these premises. Please open the door, Mr. Kovar."

No answer. They waited the required "reasonable" time, and then Jesse gestured to Nancy to unlock the door and move on. The apartment was not large or luxurious, but it was nice enough, like a middle-level motel room with a kitchenette. The living room was dark, and Camille opened the drapes to let in the sunlight and checked the window locks to be sure he hadn't escaped down the fire escape when he heard them at the door.

They searched every closet, drawer, and storage space, under the bed, inside the toilet tank—everywhere he could have hidden a knife, a wedding ring, Elisabeth Wilson's purse, or any of its contents. They put everything back the way they found it, so Capek wouldn't be alerted if he returned after they left. The apartment was clean in every sense of the word. Nancy or other housekeeping staff had made the bed and kept the rooms tidy. They found no drugs or weapons, no jewelry, nothing to indicate any illegal activities, nothing to suggest Kovar's whereabouts or past activities, no sign anybody else lived in the apartment, and no evidence of a woman's presence.

They went downstairs and thanked the desk clerk. "If Mr. Kovar comes in," Jesse told her, "don't tell him we were here. When he goes upstairs, give us a call." He handed her a card, and they went back to the Interceptor.

"He didn't have a lot of accumulated mail, so he's probably in town," Camille said. "Shall we wait and see if he shows up?"

"I want this guy so bad," he said.

"Yeah, tell me about it. I mean he's fucking rude to hotel clerks."

Jesse laughed. "She was cute too."

"Oh, please," Camille said. "Didn't I see a pizza place around here somewhere?" He pointed up the street, where they could make out a distinctive logo. "I'll buy," she said. "What would you like?"

"They have double bacon."

"I don't know how you stay in shape," she said.

"How about double bacon, green peppers, and tomatoes?"

"Okay, sounds good." Jesse tried not to remember pepperoni and extra cheese in bed with Sariah, laughing and comparing notes—she knew how to make pizza from scratch.

The pizza was hot and delicious, but the stakeout was a bust; they stayed until almost midnight and Capek never showed. They couldn't justify the expense of a round-the-clock surveillance when Capek was known to spend most of his time in Utah. All they could do was wait for a call from Richfield or the desk clerk or for a patrol officer to spot one of the vehicles.

****

They returned to the Pickett at seven a.m. to try again to serve the arrest warrant. They checked the parking lot and the nearby street parking, but found no sign of Daugherty's Camry or the Jeep. A different clerk was at the desk, and Camille didn't stop but went straight up to Room 321, while Jesse stationed himself below the fire escape. Camille knocked and called, "Housekeeping," but there was no answer.

They were back to waiting for something to break. The Richfield Police Department reported back that the address on Kovar's driver's license was not current. The post office didn't have a forwarding address, and the neighbors didn't know where he had moved. "The guy's a ghost," Camille said.

Chapter Nineteen

Three days later, after Jesse and Camille's morning had been all but consumed by paperwork, the call finally came. Patrol officers from the Traffic Division had spotted the Jeep Cherokee with Utah plates. They were hanging back, waiting for backup, and didn't think the driver was aware of them. The car was headed downtown, so Capek might have been returning home, perhaps from a trip to Utah.

Jesse and Camille were on the way in the Interceptor when the traffic cops reported on the radio that the Cherokee had made an illegal left turn. "Stupid bastard," Camille said.

Bill Forsyth, an officer Jesse knew casually, said, "We're west on Kansas Street. I'm going to pull him over."

"No!" Jesse said urgently.

"It's what I would do if there was no warrant, and if he doesn't suspect…"

"He may not know we're onto him, but he's a big guy and may be armed. Follow procedure. Wait for backup. Another unit is on its way."

"I think we can handle it," Forsyth said. "I'm pulling him over."

"Goddamn hot-doggers," Camille said. "Step on it."

Jesse kept his speed not too far over the limit, but

he was as anxious as she was. After all the slow steps to get to this point, to have the case blown by a foolhardy patrolman would be intolerable.

When they reached the scene, the Jeep Cherokee was parked on the side of the road with the patrol car behind it. The officers were another male-female team, but Bill was the more experienced officer. His partner, a slender young woman with short dark hair, stood at the driver's side door and leaned in to talk to the suspect. Officer Forsyth was about five feet behind her, checking out the back seat.

Jesse pulled in ahead of the Cherokee to be sure Capek couldn't easily escape. In the rear view mirror, he could see the female officer gesture for Capek to get out of the car. He and Camille jumped out of the Interceptor and headed back toward them.

Capek didn't comply with the instructions, and the officer repeated them. Instead of turning off the engine and getting out, he swerved toward her, but she jumped back in time. The second patrol unit drove up alongside, and his flight was aborted. More officers converged on him, and Capek got out of the car, hands raised and fingers spread in a halfhearted gesture of surrender.

He was even more formidable than Jesse had expected from his description, six foot three, about two hundred pounds of hard muscle, his hair shorter than in his mug shot, as Sariah had said, and barely touched with gray. The red scar stood out against the bulging veins in his neck. He wore denim pants and an unbuttoned black shirt over a white undershirt. He smelled of sweat and whiskey but appeared sober enough. "Hey," he said in a familiar wounded-innocent tone, "I didn't mean to hit the gas. I got rattled. All this for a wrong turn?"

Bill stepped up, very angry at what had almost happened to his partner. "Turn around and put your hands on the hood of your vehicle," he directed. "We have a warrant for your arrest."

"No, look, this is a mistake. You've got the wrong guy." He kept his hands raised, but didn't do as he was told.

"I've heard that before," Bill said. "Kazimir Zivan Capek—"

That shook him, but his bluster continued. "That's not my name. It's a mistake."

"—also known as Casey Peter Kovar, you are under arrest. Now turn around."

Scowling, Capek turned and laid his hands flat on the Jeep, but when the female cop touched his arm, he jerked it away. "Don't touch me, bitch," he snarled. "I haven't done anything. What's the charge?" Bill told him, but he continued to resist. Jesse stood ready, one hand on his holstered Glock, while the young patrolwoman used the best pain compliance method to get one arm up behind Capek's back. She and Bill had to wrestle the big man to the ground to attempt the other.

Capek lurched and jerked out of Bill's grasp, trying to get up or at least turn over. He was half on his back with the young woman's arm under him, and Bill had his Taser out, when Camille sauntered up and kicked Capek in the balls. "You just added resisting arrest," she said calmly. Most of the fight went out of him, but it still took four officers to get him handcuffed, frisked, and into the back of the patrol car.

Jesse took a deep breath of relief and shook his head at Camille. "Sometimes you go too far," he told her.

"Sometimes," she agreed. "It felt good, though."

With their suspect safely stashed, they made a quick first search of the Cherokee. The interior was as clean and uncluttered as Capek's apartment, but the glove compartment yielded a high-carbon steel knife, two rolls of duct tape, a pair of heavy work gloves, and a blackjack. The trunk held a large coil of rope and strips of cloth, which could have been used as blindfolds or gags, as well as a duffel bag and a dozen bottles of water.

****

"You don't have shit on me. This is all a bluff." Capek didn't seem as tough now, sitting in the interrogation room in handcuffs, as he had on the street.

"We have a witness who can place you next to Rosa Logan's body," Jesse told him.

"No, you don't." He was completely self-assured, quietly arrogant.

"She saw you remove Logan's wedding ring with your teeth."

His confidence slipped a bit. "She? No, she didn't. Nobody was around—and I didn't do it. You figured it out from some CSI shit. That don't make it me."

"Your DNA will. If the knife we took from your car is the murder weapon, we'll be able to prove it."

"I don't think so. I know you cops can lie about this stuff."

"Even if you cleaned it, traces of blood will show up with luminol," Jesse said. "We also know you attacked Elisabeth Wilson."

"No way. I don't even know who that is."

"Oh, I think you do. We have video of you carjacking and kidnapping her."

"No, you don't. Anyway, it don't mean I offed her."

"She doesn't remember what you did to her, but she probably will."

"She don't remember shit," Capek said. "She's dead."

"What makes you think so?"

"It was on the news."

"No, it wasn't. She survived. I've talked to her."

"Well, she's a liar."

"You're also on the hook for at least one other kidnapping. I don't have her name right now, but I will. She'll testify you threw her in the trunk of your car and dumped her on the ground in front of her husband. I'm pretty sure there were others, and we *will* find them."

Capek's manner shifted. He made a gesture of capitulation, of conceding certain facts, if not a measure of guilt. He had reached the point that so often came, when protests of innocence gave way to the desire to brag, explain, or justify. "Those bitches had it coming," he said.

"They always do," Jesse said. He had a lot of experience with the blaming of victims.

"Those weren't even their real names—they were both Jorgensen. They run off, and their old man sent me after them. Plus they stole money from him, or one of 'em did."

"He told you to kill them?"

"He said 'dead or alive'—he wasn't choosy. Then he didn't want to pay—said he was drunk and didn't mean it. He meant it, all right."

"You didn't believe he was drunk, because Mormons don't drink, right?"

"He's not a very good Mormon. Maybe he was drunk, but he meant it. He paid up in the end."

"But he didn't tell you to kill them. It was your decision."

Capek shrugged. "A man has a right to be master in his own home. Honor and obey, y'know? If he can't have 'em, nobody can. They belonged to Jorgensen. It was his call, and he said dead or alive. It's on him, not me."

"I'm afraid that's not the way it works. Killing for hire is capital murder," Jesse said. "But why not alive?"

"The first one made me work for it, pissed me off. I did the other one for fun. You probably killed people, right? You know what a rush it can be."

Jesse ignored the question. "What did you do with Logan's wedding ring?"

"It's Jorgensen, not Logan. Sent it back to her husband. It belonged to him, same as her, and it was proof I'd done it."

"What about Wilson's purse?"

"I don't know anything about it. I did what I got paid for. That's what I do."

"Why did you take Wilson to the same place?"

"Jorgensen, not Wilson." He shrugged. "Make it look like a serial killer, some crazy psycho shit."

"Very clever," Jesse said dryly. "Or maybe it was a failure of imagination. The attempted murder was hours after the kidnapping, and you transported her to the same place you killed Rosa Logan, which suggests planning, premeditation."

Capek shrugged again. "It was still early; there might have been people around. Then I heard somebody coming anyway and had to split in a hurry. I guess that's why I botched it."

"It was me," Jesse told him.

"Yeah, well, it wasn't your business, man. She was supposed to die." He shook his head in disgust. "And don't believe what *she* says. She's a liar. Told me she'd go back to Jorgensen peaceful-like and then tried to run, so I had to bash her again. Damn women, can't trust any of 'em."

"Right. But you didn't plan to take her back, did you? What happened after you put her in the car?"

Capek smirked. "We drove around for a while, and I made her suck my cock."

"You raped her," Jesse said evenly.

"No way—she belonged to Jorgensen. I wouldn't fuck another man's woman, but that don't count, and she needed to be taken down a peg. Don't think she'd ever done it before." Jesse stood up and shoved the heel of his hand hard against Capek's shoulder, just to take the smug smile off his face. He could play good cop, bad cop all by himself. "That's police brutality," Capek protested.

"Yeah, I'll show you police brutality," Jesse said and then made himself back off. He needed to stay on an even keel, and sometimes the best way to manage it was to pretend the asshole across the table from him was a human being. He supposedly had a wife, although he clearly didn't respect women. He had had a mother who must have loved him. At one time in his life he had probably loved his parents and his dog. Somewhere he had gone wrong, but he had once had the potential to be something better. And then Jesse had an odd thought: *He gave me Sariah.* In a sense, it was true. They would not have met if Capek hadn't done what he'd done. Except Jesse didn't have her. He didn't want her. She was a liar and a thief. He had lost his focus now, and he was afraid Capek could tell. "I have a better idea," he said. He went out and slammed the door for effect.

Camille was in the middle of typing a report, the tapping of the keys too steady to invite interruption. Jesse got a cup of hot, black coffee to give himself time to regroup, and then he picked up Sariah's DMV photo from his desk. Whatever had been between them was over. She was in custody. He didn't even want to know how she was faring. If she was out on bail, she had known better than to contact him. But now he remembered her cool hands on his chest. Camille's theory was downright insulting—as if a man's emotions were controlled by his hormones. Almost every conversation he'd had with Sariah had been contentious, but something so simple and peaceful had grown between them when she was lying in his arms. *Snap out of it, Aaron!*

He went back into the interrogation room and held the picture in front of Capek's face. "You know her, right?"

"No."

"Look again."

"No—I don't know who she is, but I sure as hell didn't kill her. You can't pin that one on me."

"You were her fence, weren't you?"

"Hunh? I ain't nobody's fence."

Jesse took a deep breath. "Maybe she was yours."

"I'm not a thief, man. I'm a bounty hunter."

"Stephanie Plum is a bounty hunter. You're a kidnapper and a murderer. And I hear you tried to sell some stolen chains to a warehouse employee."

"That's a load of crap. I'm not copping to that."

"But you'd like to cop to the rest, right? Write down how you tracked each of those women and took them back to Utah or wherever and how you had to kill the last two, because Jorgensen said it was okay and they asked for it?"

Capek snorted. "I guess you think I'm stupid."

"I know you're stupid. You kidnapped Wilson in front of a security camera and left your DNA in her mouth. It was clever to lie in wait at the health food store, though; I'll give you that. Use their simple desire for a familiar beverage against them. And you fooled those insurance guys too, huh? Had everybody convinced you were dead. That was smart."

"I don't know what you're talking about."

"Oh, I think you do."

"My name is Kovar. I don't know anything about that other guy."

"Your fingerprints will prove otherwise. How did you collect the checks, though?"

"I don't need to scam insurance companies. I work for a living."

"Your wife gets them, then? We were reasonably sure the present tenant didn't know anything about it. Were we wrong, or does Mrs. Capek know when they're delivered and steal them?"

"I wouldn't know."

"She won't be getting any more," Jesse said, "so I guess it doesn't matter. She'll have to pay back what she already collected, of course, and she may face charges."

Capek was annoyed, but he shrugged. "You'd have to find her first."

"We found you."

Camille opened the door. Capek took one look and said, "Keep that bitch away from me. I want my lawyer now. I want to talk to the DA. I want to make a deal."

Camille shook her head in disgust, but she left. Jesse followed her, the picture still in his hand. "He know Brennan?" she asked.

"I don't think so. He admitted almost everything else."

"I'd still like to—"

"Better not, Camille."

"Come on, I promise I won't hurt him."

"He lawyered up. Let's leave it." It felt good to have the high moral ground for a change.

****

Elisabeth looked better than on the previous visit. Her color was healthier, and she was sitting up. She still had an IV needle taped to the back of one hand, but the heart monitor had been silenced. She would be able to go home soon. "Detective Aaron," she said.

"Hi. May I?" Jesse indicated the visitor's chair.

"Please." Her voice was stronger now and less raspy.

"I wanted to let you know we have the man who did this to you in custody."

"Then I need to thank you again," she said.

"Your husband—former husband—may be arrested too, if we find sufficient evidence that he put him up to it." The possibility didn't seem to be a relief to her. Maybe it was still too much of a shock. "I want to ask you again to look at some pictures. Your assailant may or may not be among them." He put the array on the overbed tray and swung it around where she could see it. This time he got the fight-or-flight response he had hoped for before—her pupils dilated, and her breathing changed—but she shook her head.

"Nobody looks familiar?"

"No. I'm sorry."

"Please don't worry about it. We have other evidence and a confession, and it may still come back. Do you remember anything at all?"

"Settle down," she said. "I remember he told me to settle down."

"When?"

"I don't know. It's all I remember."

"It's okay." He didn't like knowing more about what had happened to her than she did, but maybe it was just as well if she didn't remember. It would be a terrible thing to face—the knowledge that somebody had done his best to end her life.

Chapter Twenty

Sariah met Jesse in the visiting room. It was small and cozy, like Olivia Maxwell's parlor, with soft green walls and comfortable furniture. Her hair was shorter, and she wore jeans and a blue T-shirt. She looked pretty damn cute. At first he only thought the color was flattering to her fair skin, but then he realized the shirt had words on the front:

I have kleptomania./ But when it gets bad,/ I take something for it!

"I knew you would come," she said.

"Don't tell me—you had a vision?" She didn't know how to respond. "Sorry… I like your shirt."

"You have to be able to laugh at yourself." She gestured toward the small couch against the wall, and he followed her and sat down when she did, not too close. "I do, you know," she said.

"What?"

"Take something. Medication, not merchandise. It's supposed to help me control my impulses. The first one we tried made me sleepy all the time. I'm told this one has sexual side effects, but it's not a problem right now. It makes me feel sick sometimes, but they say it will pass. I hate having to take it."

"They can't force you," he said. "You can refuse."

She shook her head. "I say, 'Yes sir.' That was your advice, remember? You gave me good advice;

that's why I'm here instead of prison."

"You know you can still go to prison?"

"Yes, I understood the deferred sentencing agreement. Thank you for helping me."

"I didn't do much."

"Yes, you did. You told the prosecutor I was your CI."

"I told them you helped us. I didn't say you were my CI. That was Vince. He's a good guy."

"He told me he went through the police academy with you. He told me some other things too."

"Uh-oh," he said. It was easier to talk to her than he'd expected it would be.

"How is C.C.?" she asked.

"Doing great. I get his seed from World of Wings. The owner asked about you."

"How embarrassing. I don't know what I'm going to do when I get out of here. I'll never be able to work in retail again. I'm sorry about the art gallery job. I would have enjoyed it."

"There are other kinds of jobs," Jesse said.

"They say they'll help me find one, but being on probation will make it hard. I guess I'll have to become a movie star. They get forgiven for almost everything."

"You're pretty enough."

She smiled and brushed her hair back from her face. "For a white girl, you mean?"

"Maybe I'm not too particular."

"Watch out or I'll have to go off my meds. That was a joke."

"How are you doing in here? Besides the side effects?"

"It's okay," she said, but she sounded a little grim.

"Very institutional, you know, but everybody's nice. They want to help. My therapist, Dr. Lang, is a decent guy. Stodgy, but decent."

"Is he helping you?"

"Maybe. He listens to me, and then I listen to him and say, 'Yes, sir.'"

"I've created a monster," he said.

"My roommate is messy, and she snores. Other than that…I miss…lots of things." She didn't look at him when she said it, and then she met his eyes and asked, "Are you visiting me as a friend, or is this another interrogation?"

"I came to see you," he said, "but I wouldn't mind knowing a couple of things. How did you know Capek was at the warehouse? Were you there, or did you have a vision, or…?"

She sighed. "Which would you prefer? I'm tired of trying to figure it out."

"I'd prefer the truth."

She studied him gravely. "It wasn't a vision—that would be something seen. I didn't hear voices like Joan of Arc either. I just knew. I had no doubt about it. Absolute certainty. It was the same when my brother fell in the well. Maybe it only happens when a life is at stake. If you don't believe me, then don't."

She had said the same thing about the polygamy story, and it was apparently true. He was too much of a rationalist to accept her explanation, but he wouldn't ask again. Would it make any real difference if she admitted she had seen Capek when Elisabeth was attacked? "Okay," he said.

"Is it? What else did you want to know?"

"Rosa Logan and Elisabeth Wilson changed their

names when they relocated. Did you? Idaho doesn't have any records on you."

"And you would have checked, wouldn't you? You can understand why we'd want to stay under the radar. Most of the women don't drive, and the children are born at home or at the local clinic. Even in Mackay I never used the name Smith. The women who got new identities had to hide from their husbands. I didn't. He won't come after me."

"Would you ever go back?"

"Never. I didn't need a new name, but I needed help to start my new life."

"You didn't change your name because it's who you are—and so Anna could find you if she needed to?"

"Don't talk about Anna." Her expression didn't change, and she sat passively with her hands in her lap.

"I'm sorry, Sariah…really, I'm sorry." He touched her hand and couldn't resist moving closer. "I'm sorry if it seems like I'm cross-examining you. I didn't mean to act like a cop. The last thing I want is to make you feel bad."

"I'm doing a lot of that—apologizing, not feeling bad. Well, that too. I have to do the twelve-step thing, write letters of apology to all the stores and people I stole from. I'm sorry I took your cufflinks. Did you get them back?"

"Yes. Should I be glad you didn't take the Keurig as well?" He smiled to take the sting out of the question.

She put a hand against his chest, as if to preserve the distance between them, but her fingers lingered. "I never saw my husband completely undressed," she said, "but I know he wasn't like you. Your body was so amazing to me, and not just what it could make me feel. The muscles, the color of your skin—like beautiful polished wood. If you were a piece of sculpture, I would have shoplifted you." She leaned in and brushed her lips against his.

"I don't think your meds are working," he said.

Sariah gave a shaky laugh and took her hand away. "This is not the place," she said. "I know you'll find someone else, someone better, but maybe we could be friends." Before he could answer, she asked, "Can you stay for lunch?"

"It's not against the rules?"

"No, it's fine. It's not Quique's—it's only a cafeteria—but the food isn't awful."

"All right. Awful is what I usually have for lunch."

She smiled. "They tell me the coffee isn't bad, but I haven't tried it."

"Next time I'll bring you a jar of Postum," he said. "Is that allowed?"

"Gifts of food? Yes. It would be lovely. Will there be a next time?" She was relieved now, and her cheeks had more color.

He didn't answer—it depended on how this visit went. "I like your hair," he said instead.

"You do? It's easier to take care of." She glanced through the window, where he could see a green lawn and a few trees. "Is it nice out? We could walk on the grounds and then go to lunch. It's less crowded if you go early."

"All right."

They headed outside. It was a fine spring day, sunny and cool, and the grounds were pleasant enough, an ornamental garden surrounded by a wall, which needn't have been for security. A well-worn path curved under the trees where a few people—Inmates? Patients? Residents?—sat in wicker chairs. Jesse and Sariah strolled along it, close but not touching, and she greeted a couple of people by name but didn't introduce him.

After a few minutes of silence—not strained, but not entirely comfortable—Jesse said, "Do you remember what you said before we were together the first time?" She shook her head.

"You said you wanted to trust me. I want to trust you, Sariah."

"It's what I want too, but I know how hard it is for you, after all that's happened."

"It only comes with hearing the truth."

"You know all my secrets now. The rest is up to you."

Jesse took her slender, warm hand in his and they walked on. He had come here hoping for some degree of closure. This felt more like a beginning.

A word about the author...

Linda Griffin retired as Fiction Librarian for the San Diego Public Library to spend more time on her writing, and her stories have been published in numerous journals.

In addition to the three R's—reading, writing, and research—she enjoys Scrabble, movies, and travel.

Guilty Knowledge is her third romance from the Wild Rose Press.

Visit her at:
http://www.lindagriffinauthor.com/

Thank you for purchasing
this publication of The Wild Rose Press, Inc.

For questions or more information
contact us at
info@thewildrosepress.com.

The Wild Rose Press, Inc.
www.thewildrosepress.com